The Epic Saga of Razzle, Dazzle and Gustov

By

Arsidious, The Great Writer

These books are an Experiment in Error: they are an exploration and a celebration of all the mistakes people make in creating great lit. I apologize in advance.

Zarqnon the Embarrassed.

[leave this page blank for reader to take extensive notes]

Razzle Find a Magic Ring!

By

Arsidious The Great Writer

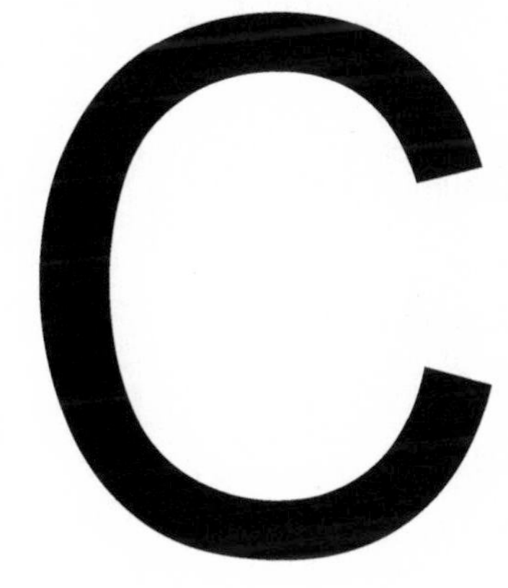

hapter 1

One magical day, Dazzle, Razzle, and Gustov decided to get out of their condo and go to the grocery store because they were out of food and they needed something to eat or they would all starve like crazy while watching t.v. when they all got home from a hard days work where they spent their day earning money to pay for all their magical adventures.

While packing up to go to the store, Dazzle said, "can we wait one minute? I was inspired by something I saw on the news!"

"What was the news about?" said Razzle.

"I don't really remember," said Dazzle. "Just remember seeing this really cool movie poster in the background with a picture of a frog and a pig and a bear."

"Woah, that is so cool!" said Gustov. "What was the movie about?"

"I think it was about the stock market," said Dazzle.

"Well, let's hear your piece of master!" said Razzle.

"Yes! We anxiously away the gentle words of your prose."

So Dazzle took the paper, struck a pose, took a breath, and poured out words.

"Come, sweet street of walls
Paint your path as it ever calls
Words of zest and quails
Leptons and fezziwigs, gummies and gum-
balls

The frogs and pigs dance in the lake
It's closer than farther and always awake
Tether and weather, soup and steak

Its breath it echoes like an earthquake.

So come one, come few
It won't be like what it will be when it's through
The chalice and the platter are harder to chew
The grids and the graphs find it harder to skew

They heckle and hackle
Jeckle and Jackle
Pickle and Packle
Wickle and Duck Sauce

"That's all I have for now," Dazzle said putting the paper down.

"That was extraordinary!" said Razzle. "It is a work like no other!"

"To add another word would be to taint it's bustling beauty!" said Gustov.

"Thank you!" said Dazzle. "Your undying

support means everything to me!"

"On that note, we need to hurry up if we are going to catch the trolly!" said Razzle.

"Yes, let's head out for the door, lest we are late!" said Gustov.

While at the bus stop, Razzle said, "my pockets are so heavy. When I went to the bank to cash my hard earned check that I worked long and hard for, they told me they had just ran out of dollars, so they would have to pay me with quarters up until the amount was less than 25 cents, in which they would have to pay me with dimes up until the amount was less than 10 cents, then they would have to use a nickel and some pennies, up until the value remaining was less than a cent, and then they would deposit it in some cryptocurrency account."

"That's very wise of them," said Gustov. "You never know where the crypto market is going to go. Maybe some day those fractions of pennies will turn into zillions of dollars! And then we could buy an island and start our own candle soap franchise pyramid where we make candles out of soap so people can have a candle in the shower they can use."

"That...would....be...AWESOME!" said Dazzle as he finished off his bologna and peanut butter sandwich.

Chapter 2

Right then, after waiting 57 minutes, because the bus was on a 45 minute loop schedule and they just missed the last bus because they were busy playing tiddlywinks behind the trees, the bus pulled up. As it came to a stop, they read on the side of the bus a new sign that said "new policy: whole dollars only. We are having trouble keeping up with the coins."

Razzle said "oh no! I only have coins! What ever will I do?!?"

Gustov said "well, maybe we could walk! The store is just across the street!"

Dazzle said "But then we would have to cross the street! How will we be able to do that safely?!?"

Razzle said "well, we could walk down to

Razzle said “well, we could walk down to that corner over there! There is a crossing guard there, and I am betting if we wait long enough, some children going to school will come by and we could cross with them when the crossing guard gives them the OK!”

So everyone went over to the corner and waited.

And they made it just in time, as a group of kids with their parents were heading across the street to school.

As they went into the store, Razzle spotted the quarter prize machines on the wall.

Razzle said “oh goodness! I have always loved getting magical surprises from these mystical machines!”

So Razzle put in a quarter, turned the twisty knob, and pulled out a bouncy rubber ball.

“Oh joy of all joys! I have wanted one of these for the longest time, since i have recently lost my favorite one in the whole world when I bounced it and it hit a crack in the sidewalk and flew up into the air, hit a tree branch, and landed in a passing by garbage truck."

So Razzle walked home a happy Razzle with a new bouncy ball.

But when Razzle examined it closer, a scream came out.

"Hey, everyone! This ball has the initial R on it like my old ball did. Do you think this could actually be my old ball?"

"I don't know!" said Dazzle. "Maybe it is!"

"Maybe some ancient spirit took it from our house to keep it safe until such a time that we needed it!" said Gustov.

"Sounds plausible!" said Razzle. While drinking looking at a poster of the trio's favorite movie, Razzle accidently dropped the ball into the coffee cup Dazzle sat on the table.

“Oh no!” said Dazzle. “That is going to completely change the texture of my coffee!”

But as Razzle’s fingered fished around in the coffee mug to find the ball, Razzle pulled out a magic mood ring.

“A magic mood ring!” said Gustov. “It must have been hiding in the ball and was exposed when the ball dissolved in the coffee!”

“I wonder what it does!” Dazzle says taking another sip of coffee.

“I don’t know!” said Razzle as the ring is slipped on Razzle’s pointer finger. Razzle disappears.

“Where did Razzle go?!?” said Dazzle.

“Razzle was just here!!!!” said Razzle.

“I am still here!” said Razzle. “Can’t you see me?”

“Oh no!” said Dazzle. “It must make you invisible!”

"Take it off before you disappear forever!" said Gustov.

Chapter 4

Razzle took off the ring.

"Try it on a different finger!" said Dazzle.

"Yes, maybe it does something different on different fingers!" said Gustov.

"Ok." said Razzle as the ring is slipped on the middle finger. Everyone gasped as Razzle started floating in the air.

"Woah!" said Dazzle.

"Try another finger!" said Gustov.

"Ok." said Razzle. Razzle slipped the ring

“Ok.” said Razzle. Razzle slipped the ring on the ring finger. Then, wham bam pow, there were multiple Razzles all over the room.

“It must be a duplicator cloning move to confuse people who are attacking us!” said Dazzle.

“Or a way of getting extra help with cleaning the RV.” said Gustov. “We could have a couple of them function as sous chefs!”

As Dazzle finished the cup of coffee, a note was sitting on the bottom of the cup. “There must have been a note in ball, too!”

“Awesome!” Said Gustov. “Maybe it was dehydrated and the coffee rehydrated it.”

“What does it say?” said Razzle.

Dazzle took the poem, written on an ancient napkin, hidden in the rubber ball.

“Take the ring from inside the ball

Bash it against the wall
But when the ball in the coffee falls
The answers for everything will come to all

The thumb the answer to all of the secrets
Answers to questions off all the tests
Tests that lead us to the knowledge best
Just take the winnebago and head west

Drop the ring in the fires of Valhalden Pond
A pond of lava that opens the door to the beyond
A land you will find so fond
When the ring is destroyed and turned into a wand."

"How do we turn the ring into a wand?" said Gustov.

"Simple!" said Razzle. "We take it and like it said: stick it in lava, and it will turn into a wand."

Dazzle said "where is this lava?"

"How would I know?" said Gustov.

Then Razzle slipped it on the thumb. A portal opened up and a clunky intergalactic winnebago popped out, and a strange green frog jumped out and said “anyone looking for a ride?”

“Ohhh, I always wanted to ride in a winnebago!” said Razzle.

“Me too!” said Dazzle.

“What is a winnebago?” Said Gustov?”

“It is the intergalactic vehicle of choice!” said Nuhamshur. “I inherited this from my parental units, and they inherited it from their parental units!”

“Awesome!” said Gustov. “I had no idea that there was a vehicle especially designed for galactic travel!”

“Can we go on a ride?” said Dazzle.

“Yes, may we?” said Razzle.

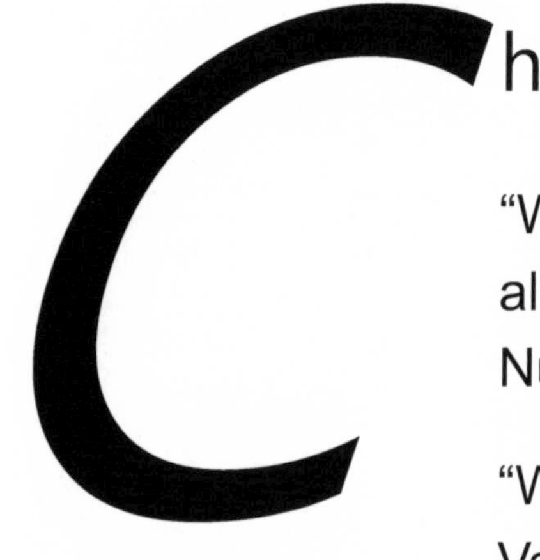

hapter 5

"Where would you all like to go?" said Nuhamshur.

"We are looking for Valhalden Pond. do you know where it is?" asked Dazzle.

"I think it is out west somewhere in the galaxy." said Nuhamshur. "I used to go there when I was a tadpole and swim."

"That sounds awesome." said Razzle. "But I don't think we brought our swimsuits."

"That's alright," said Nuhamsur. "It's mostly lava now, so you probably wouldn't want to go swimming."

"You make a very valid point!" said Gustov.

hapter 6

"I think we all need to calm down and head on if we are going to make it back before our favorite shows at the theatre come on." said Razzle.

"Yes, I think we all just need to chill and head on." said Dazzle. "You all are the wind beneath my arms!"

“Aw, that is so awesome!” said Nuhamsur. “I wish I shared that comradery with someone.”

“Well, you can be our friend.” said Razzle.

“Yes,” said Dazzle. “We can always use another friend, our *lagun arraroa ileorde bitxi batekin*!”

“Oh yes! “ said Gustov. “You can help us when we rotate the light bulbs. We have found that if we rotate light bulbs, it helps them last longer. We got the idea when they were rotating the tires on the bus. We found out they were rotating the tires one day when it was really late.”

“Awesome!” said Nuhamsur. “Now lets head to Valhalden Pond. Vacation awaits us!”

“WAIT!” said Gustov.

“What is it?” said Dazzle.

“Did we forget the backgammon board?” said Razzle.

“No!” said Gustov.

“The wild safari trading cards?” said Nuhamsur.

“No! But we should take those just in case.” said Gustov.

“Our old marbles?” said Dazzle.

“YES!” said Razzle. “We need our marbles! We never know when we might need them”

So Razzle goes back into the house and comes back with a bag of marbles.

EVerybody jumps on the bus.

The bus takes off down the road.

The rockets come out of the back.

They ignite.

The bus takes off into the air.

Everybody screams.

Gustov drops the marbles.

Everyone cries a little.

Gustov picks them up.

Everybody appreciates Gustov for picking them up.

Dazzle spilled some coffee.

The bus enters the stratosphere.

Everybody gasps.

They all agree it's beautiful.

Nuhamsur takes a left heading east.

Everybody reminds Nuhamsur the pond is west.

Nuhamsur assures them the GPS is showing east.

Everybody shows Nuhamsur the GPS is up-side down.

Nuhamsur realizes that's why the winnebego arrived on Earth and not planet Hortntort.

“I have been driving with it upside-down this entire time!” cried Nuhamsur.

“That’s alright,” said Dazzle. “One I forgot to cover the salad in the refrigerator and the lettice got all wilted.”

“And once I built and entire water capacitor thingamabob and then realized I used the completely wrong color lego.” said Razzle.

“And once, Razzle and Dazzle used all the pastel glitter, so when it came time for me to do my project, I was sad.” said Gustov.

“I understand,” said Nuhamsur. “It just that I have never had friends before, and if I didn’t accidentally turn it upside-down, I would have never met you!”

“But you were destined too!” said Razzle. “It said so in the note I found in my bouncy ball!"

"I guess you are right." said Nuhamsur.

"Can we stop by the drive through?" said Dazzle. "I need a drink."

"OK." said Nuhamsur.

When they got to the drive through, every-body ordered their drink.

When they got to the window, the attendant said "we can't take coins. Our coin container is at the coin container cleaning company because it has some dirt on it."

"Well, I am out of dollars." said Razzle.

"I am too" said Nuhamsur.

"I am as well" said Dazzle.

"Well, I have no more dollars either." said Gustov.

Everyone started to cry.

Chapter 7 & 8

“Well, do you have any marbles?” said the attendant?

“Why, yes!” said Razzle. “We do have marbles!”

“Why marbles?” puzzled Dazzle.

“Because, the Gubnub Galaxy on Gordon Grove, in which we are corporately headquartered, marbles are the new crypto currency because we can digitize them and trade them on the Gordon Grove Galaxy Stock Exchange.” said the attendant.

“Hey!” said Nuhamsur. “Did you used to have a relative that played in a band in the Frufrit galaxy circuit?”

“Why, yes!” said the attendant. “I am the lead bass player, and the rest of my relatives play the theremin.”

“I never played a bass made out of lead before!” said Gustov.

“It sounds quite heavy!” said Razzle.

“Like a heavy metal bass!” said Dazzle.

“Well, fortunately, the gravity on Frufit is really an anti-gravity, so the heavier things are lighter there, and the lighter things are incredibly heavy," said Shirquill.

"Can I join your band?" said Nuhamsur. "I have never been in a band, and I have a winnebego for touring!"

"That would be awesome!" said Shirquill.

"Sorry, but I won't be able to take you to the pond today," said Nuhamsur. "I need to practice for my next gig."

"We are sorry to see you go," said Dazzle.

"Yes, but we are glad you found some friends," said Razzle.

"And we are glad you found your purpose in life," said Gustov.

So the trio grabs a bus back home - one that took coins - happy their new found friend found a good band to belong to.

"I wonder what instrument Nuhamsur plays," said Dazzle.

“I think Nuhamsur looks like a clarinet player,” said Razzle.

“I always wanted to learn to play the Pan-Flute,” said Gustov.

Everyone agreed that would be neat as they headed home for lunch.

“I wonder what would happen if I put the ring on my other hand.” said Razzle.

“or if you put it on your toes!” Said Dazzle.

“Or wore it like a necklace!” said Gustov.

Razzle looked for the ring. It was gone. In Razzle’s pocket was a note. It said:

Chance is the wind upon which we sail
Art is the dream upon we prevail
Life is the ride of the fading pale
we write the script of the passing whale

Taste the light as it flutters by
wait for the moth as it sails through the sky
quest for the morrow in the panda’s eye

E END

Stay tune for the next exciting adventure of Razzle, Dazzle, and Gustov!

Dazzle finds a map in the newspaper!

By

Arsidious The Great Writer

One day, Razzle, Dazzle, and Gustov were sitting around the table. Razzle was reading the paper he bought from a guy standing outside the grocery store. The guy said it was a special newspaper from the future. But honestly, it just had the regular news. Dazzle was working on a poem, and Gustov was eating a 3 day old biscuit he didn't finish eating from a value meal he got on the way home from the doctor.

Dazzle said "anyone know a word that rhyme with 'blue'"?

Razzle and Gustov paused.

"Voo doo with an emu" replied Razzle'

"Boo Boo on my canoe" replied Gustov.

"Goo Goo over kung fu" replied Razzle.

"A new kazoo from Kathmandu" replied Gustov

"Misconstrue the Overview" replied Razzle.

"New Zoo review" replied Gustov

"Gary Gnu" replied Razzle.

"Born in a bijou" replied Razzle.

"A sad cebu" replied Gustov

"Who made you?" replied Razzle.

"Who are *you?" replied Gustov*

"Well, kuzah, I'm Dazzle!" said Dazzle. "I thought you knew that, Gustov".

"I was just replying to your question, Dazzle" said Gustov. "there is no reason to get all wound up!"

"Calm down!" said Razzle, sipping his coffee. "There is no reason for everyone getting wounded up!"

Razzle then said "what are you working on, Dazzle?" and Dazzle said "a poem". Gustov said "can you read it to us?" and Dazzle said "O.K."

Dazzle paused for a moment. And then Dazzle started to read.

Can I conundrum
the wind beneath the fire escape
without tickling the sun

Can I obfuscate
The water within the goal
posts
With making the camel laugh

Can I emundate
The crystal salad plate
With the finest of glitter glue

Time is the creak
That runs through the backyard
without permission
And erodes the foundations
of everything immortalized

I am still waiting
for the last train to nowhere
to stop and pick me up
And take me there

Towards the end of the rainbow
lays a walrus
who just wants to know
when the stars are going to dance

Alas the gobbly gook
has finally broken the mouse's back
Shoe string, tether me a lace upon
which to store my broken imagination

Why do the Flavors not blend quite like I
imagine.
Fluffleberry
Cornstacking Cognitive Dissonance
upon Wet noodles
Skwabulousness

Dazzle put down the paper. "I am lost at where I should go from there."

"AS IF!" said Gustov. "I think it is just perfect as it is!"

Razzle put down his newspaper and started clapping. "Why, I think it is most excellent, dear Dazzle! I think we should post it on the internet! Maybe everyone will read it, and it will go viral, and we shall become filthy rich! Rich! Rich, I say!"

Gustov said “but if we become filthy rich, will I still be able to eat peanut butter and banana sandwiches every other Tuesday?”

Chapter 2

Dazzle said “I guess. Didn’t Elvis eat those even after he became famous?”

Razzle, Dazzle, and Gustov stopped what they were doing and pondered. After they pondered for a moment, they went back to what they were previously doing. “Maybe Elvis had to change to Wednesday when he at them,” said Razzle.

“But Wednesday is pancake day! And we can’t do anything that would endanger pancake day” said Dazzle.

“But not ever Wednesday,” said Razzle. “Sometimes we eat Falafel. Maybe we could switch out falafel day for something else, so we could eat our PB&B sandwiches on alternating Wednesdays we are not eating pancakes.”

After his last bite of his 3 day old biscuit, Gustov said “I wonder what we will do today”. All of a sudden, something dropped out of Razzle’s paper.

“What is that?” said Dazzle. “I don’t know.” said Razzle. Gustov picked it up and opened it.

“It has lots of lines and strange markings” said Gustov.

“It must be a map for a hidden treasure” said Razzle.

Dazzle said “What is the location of the treasure?”

“I don’t know” said Gustov. “There is a big greasy smudge mark where the X is. Like someone was eating a biscuit and didn’t wipe their hands.

Razzle picked up a comb and tried to wet down a lose cowlick. “Maybe we should go see if we could find it. Then we could get rich and buy that food processor we always wanted.”

Dazzle said “As if! That would be the best thing ever!”

Gustov said “I know, right? Then we could process our own food!”

Razzle said “Like smoothies and guacamole dip!”

“or even make our own peanut butter! Or Salad Dressing! Or tapioca pudding!” said Dazzle.

Everybody agreed that would be the best thing ever.

They cleaned up the house and wiped down the ceiling fan for excessive dust, and then headed out the apartment door. Dazzle made sure to change the voice machine to let everyone know they were simply running around the apartment, drinking vitamin water, baking zitis, and rummaging through old photo albums, because he didn't want to give anyone the impression they were really out hunting a humongous motherload of pirate lost bullion.

Chapter 3

They left a note on the door that they would be out for a few years searching for treasure, and if anyone needed them, they could reach them on their social media site, BaseCook. Razzle invented BaseCook when he went to culinary school in France to become a famous pastry chef. His favorite food was Hot Dogs - he liked beef, but would eat the kind with pork, turkey, and mystery meat in it as well. but he thought it was fun to make cookies, and a great way to get famous and rich at the same time.

As they headed for the parking garage, Dazzle realized he forgot the car keys. So he went back to the apartment. While there, he made some tapioca pudding to take with him, in case he got hungry.

It took forever to find the car. Apparently Gustov took it to the mall and didn't park it in their usual spot, 3 slots over from the elevator on the seventh floor. To his defense, somebody had taken his spot. 2 weeks later they closed down the seventh to make room for the new laundromat, since the other one on the second floor burned down to the ground when a rabbit caused an electrical fire.

ground when a rabbit caused an electrical fire.

They finally found the car parked across the street at the art museum where Gustov likes to stare at the abstract things. Unfortunately, it had a boot on it because a van hit it from behind and pushed it 3 inches over the parking line into a loading zone. Gustov called his friend Randolph to take care of it, since it was Randolph's car, and because Gustov forgot to fill it back up with gas and it was on empty.

Fortunately, the bus was running 15 minutes behind schedule, otherwise they would have missed it and had to wait a whole 45 minutes or else find a taxi. They could have called Chadwick, but they were afraid Chadwick would want to come along and bring his pet iguana. Iguanas make horrible treasure hunting pets. They get in fights with Dazzle's pet li

So everyone hopped on the bus. Razzle had trouble getting his ultimate hiking backpack on the bus, because it was so heavy from all the stuff he carried in it. It is one of the reasons they didn't walk to the treasure, because it was so heavy. Razzle carried everything from his old Happy Days water bottle, He-man lunch box, a couple of cassette tapes in case they need something to listen to, a George Foreman grill, an etch-a-sketch for on-the-go drawings, and a plethora of other essentials. It was a good thing he had it, because no sooner than when they got on the bus, Dazzle said "my thumb hurts. I think I have a boo boo." so Razzle went to action, pulling out an exclusive

Snooky bandage and saved the day. They were like Snoopy, but specially made in Botswana. Dazzle said “thanks”, and Gustov said “that was a close one. It is a good thing we came prepared. Here is a chewy granola bar with blueberries.” Dazzle said “No thanks. I just had some cheese puffs.” He was always told it would behoove him to say “no thanks”. Saying “thanks” and “no thanks” was proper manners and it made people happy. His uncle didn’t say “thanks” and “no thanks”, and it always made people in the family uncomfortable at his lack of couth.

When we got on the bus, the driver looked at us suspiciously. He had a Twinkie on the dash and a twinkly in his eye and a winkle in his nose and a smirkle on his mouth. Gustov said “watch out guys, I think the driver may be up to something!”

The bus was suspiciously empty except for one person reading a newspaper and another person sitting next to a huge box that looked like it could hold a refrigerator. Both people kept their faces hidden so noone could see what they looked like. But then Razzle said “look! That person is reading the newspaper upside-down!” But Gustov replied “that is because it is folded over. It’s simply physics.”

Gustov replied, “oh. OK. I understand.”

Then Dazzle turned and said “I wonder what is in that box. Do you think they might have some cream puffs in there?”

“I don’t know,” said Razzle. “Maybe you should go

over there and ask."

So Dazzle stood up to go ask. But right as he got to the box, a bunch of screaming Koala looking aliens broke through the window and started screaming really loud.

"OH NO!" screamed Gustov. "I think those cute little bears got hurt breaking through the windows! Quick, Razzle! The Snoopy bandaids!"

But Dazzle interjected. "Koalas are not technically bears. Genetically, they are semi-quadrupedal arboreal herbivorous marsupials belonging to the Vombatidae family and are closer related to wombats."

Gustov said inquisitively "I thought the Vombatidae family was from Sheboygan, which I used to think was in Michigan, but just recently learned was in Wisconsin."

Dazzle said "you must have been thinking of Cheboygan, which is in Michigan. Sheberghan is in Afghanistan."

Then Razzle rubbed his belly and said "I really could go for some Chef Boyardee Spaghetti ohs."

While contemplating how delicious a plate of Spaghetti-os would be, several of the koala aliens - or koalalians - started spraying canned cheese over everything. The koalalians started going "gibbly gibbly gibbly". Gustov pulled out his universal translator and said "I think that means 'yummy, yummy yummy, I can't wait to eat everything here with cheese all over it.' "

Dazzle said "oh no! Not canned cheese! That's the worst! It never comes out of my hair!"

Razzle replied "not only that, it will ruin my watch!"

Gustov added "not only that, but if they use all the canned cheese, what will we put on corn? Ketchup?"

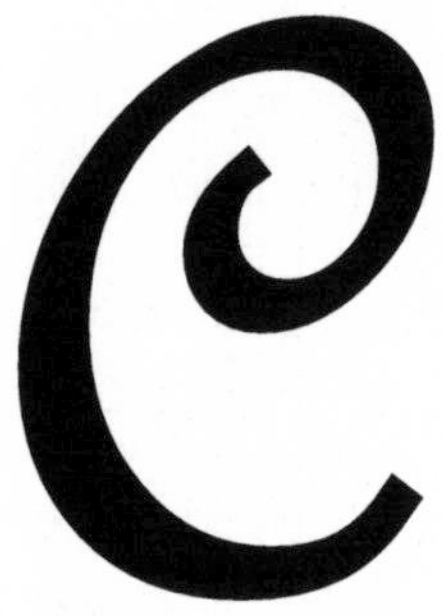

hapter 5

As the Koalalians ate the seats covered in canned cheese, canned cheese was making the Koalalians get larger and crazier. And the larger and crazier they got, the more they ate. And the more they ate, the larger and crazier they got.

Razzle said “I have an idea! Do you have your ketchup, Gustov?”

Gustov said “I might have a few packets left over from lunch. Why, what are you thinking?”

Dazzle said “I see where you are going. Maybe if we go down town, we could get some soft pretzels and use my leftover ketchup!”

Razzle said “as good as that sounds, maybe we could first spay ketchup on everything and maybe the ketchup will counter the canned cheese and cause the Koalalians to develop a craving for

cause the Koalalians to develop a craving for pretzels and they will head down town. And maybe the salt on the pretzels will make them thirsty, and they will go try to get some sodas, but when they realize they don't have enough change, they will go back to the planet Tucson."

So Dazzle sprayed ketchup on a chair. When the Koalaliens ate the ketchup, a third eye popped out of their heads. They went "skrub skrub." Gustov said "the universal translator said they need more ketchup or they will eat everything the whole district."

While Razzle, Dazzle, and Gustov were shivering in their timbers, the large refrigerator box popped open, and 3 magic fish named Benrabbakan, Shanadabawingit, and Zeb flew out. And with their lazer eyes, they hypnotized the Koalaliens. They said "come and follow us". So the Koalaliens followed the magic fish as they explored the universe.

"That was close," said Razzle. "I know," said Dazzle. "I really thought we were goners" said Gustov. Then, the person dropped the newspaper. It was a ghost from the planet Gooberon. The ghost said "You were never in any danger. We have been watching you."

Dazzle said "who is this 'we'". The person behind the box stood up. It was a ghost, too. Razzle said "there are two of them!"

They said "we are here to take you to the

treasure."

The driver hit a button, and the bus turned into a magic ghost ship that could travel through any dimension. The first place they went was Planet Tucson to make sure the Koalaliens made it home safely. Next, they had to go to Gooberon so the ghosts could check on the kids and make sure they weren't getting into any trouble.

After making sure all the ghost children were fed and put to bed, the crew headed off.

"Wee!" said Gustov.

"This is so fun!" said Razzle.

"I haven't done anything like this before!" yelled Dazzle.

"I know!" said Razzle. "It's like a great big roller coaster without tracks!"

"Or like an airplane without wings!" said Gustov.

"We need to make sure to put on our seatbelts!" said Dazzle. "We haven't been doing that since we left, and that is not good!"

"Sorry, Dazzle!" said Razzle. "I guess we forgot!"

"What if we were in a crash and didn't have our seatbelts! Then it would be all our fault!" they said together.

So everyone put on their seatbelts, except for the

two ghosts.

“You need to put on your seatbelts!” said Dazzle. “What kind of example are you setting if you do not put them on properly!”

“I guess you are right!” said the ghosts as they put their seatbelts on.

While they were flying the speed of light through the universe, Dazzle said “Hey, while we are waiting to land, do any of you want to hear a poem I wrote?”

“Sure” said Razzle.

“Absolutely” said the ghosts.

“Maybe we can pop some popcorn while we listen!” said Gustov.

Everybody went “yum!” in unison, except for the bus driver. The bus driver said “no thank you. I am driving, and it is not a good practice to eat while you are driving. I am also out of napkins and am afraid I would get popcorn juice all over the steering wheel. Another bus driver did that several days ago, and it was really yucky.”

“That is very responsible of you!” said Gustov. “I am sorry you had to drive with a yucky steering wheel. If I had known, I would have brought some wippies.”

“Wait!” said Razzle. “I think there are some Snurf wippies in the backpack! I saw them there when I was putting in the cheese cake!"

"That is awesome!" said Dazzle. "Now our bus driver won't have to drive with a yucky steering wheel."

Walking a shallow road
of the fragile porcelain
slightly intricately changes
one's point of perception

Pencil shaped Pencils
Scribe on paper made sheets of paper
Forming shapes that look like letters
That echo thought formed thoughts

Flob-nob
Wally-walter Wallace
Fibble-nib
Polly-Palter palace

For all the engraved polyhedrons
I have laid my eyes upon
and spilt my trapezoids
on the bow.

I challenge my most inner being
That I might find favor
With flavor of chip
no one dares to speak of

Squigle me
a plaid doormat
Dormant
and delightful

Oh no, said the Ferryman
I appear to have lost my cheesecake
And with that, the circus was nevermore
No one the wiser

"That was the most excellent thing my ears have ever encountered!" said the ghost with a newspaper.

Chaper 6

"Thank you very much!" said Dazzle. Would you like to hear another?"

"Oh yes, please!" said the ghost behind the box.

> Lah
> Lah bah dah
> Lab bah, dah bah, zing
> Willi nilly winni zoo
>
> Doh
> Doh goh boh
> Doh goh, boh dah, kip
> Du gaa gu dah zinki Woo
>
> Foo
> Foo Fa Lum
> Foo Fa Lum fizzy
> Ra la la ba da
>
> Vrum
> Vruhm Vroom Vram
> Vruhm Vroom Vram Viki icky

Din va doo

"I like it, but I didn't understand a word of it" said Gustov.

"Oh, I understood every word of it" said the driver. "It was written in my mother tongue, Goobernese. It sounds very much like a poem my nana-geist used to read to me. Not exact. There are enough differences to make it your own and keep anyone from thinking you plagiarized it."

"Thank you!" said Dazzle. "I am glad you appreciate my desire to make it my own but still capture the essence of your culture."

The bus driver pulls into a driveway in an old abandoned house on a planet far away from where Gustov, Dazzle, and Razzle live. Razzle looked at the map and said "I think we are really close to where the treasure is."

The driver said "I think so to. Here is where I drop you guys off. School is about to let out, and I have to go take the children home."

So Razzle, Gustov, and Dazzle, along with their two new ghost friends, got off the bus and headed for the house. When they got to the house, the door was locked.

"Oh no! How will we ever get in?" said Gustov.

"If only we knew someone that could pass through the walls and unlock it from the other

Dazzle finds a map in the newspaper!

The End

Note: put some graphics or pictures on these pages later so they aren't so blank

Book 3

Gustov Finds a Key that Opens a Portal!

By

Arsidious, The Great Writer

Razzle, Dazzle, and Gustof were sitting around the table. Razzle was reading the morning paper. Dazzle was writing some poetry. And Gustof was eating leftover pizza.

After his second bite, Gustof said "my pizza is still not hot enough. The pineapple is fine, but the anchovies are cold like small salty fishes that haven't been warmed enough in the microwave, which is sad, because the anchovies have so much promise if the were nice and warm with the warmiestness to go in collusion with the overly spoken saliness of the fish."

Razzle said "What are you writing, Dazzle?"

"A very important poem" said Dazzle.

"What is it about," said Gustof.

It is it about the great conflict between the Rockitage and the Paperitage and the Scissoritage and after years of futile fighting, they were united in a new struggle when the Lizarditage and the Spockitiage invaded them." Dazzle Replied.

"It sounds most exquisite" said Razzle. "Can we hear it?"

"o.k." said Dazzle.

Gustof grabbed his pizza from the microwave and handed everyone a piece as they listened to Dazzle's new masterpiece.

behold the grand Rockitage
who fight and argue with the Paperitage
who nash and quarrel with the Scissoritage
over the land country of Wisconitage

Slashing and a bashage
Covering and gashage
The fighting and gnashage
Never ending, Never ceasingage

Ever until one night of all nightage
in the middle of Fights of all fightage

they are interjected by the Lizarditage
and intercepted by the Spocketage

they said "this is our heritage
dancing like rabid savages
I would love a chicken salad sandwiches
to feed to my finches

nanu nanu nanitage
yaba daba yabatage
Snork snork snorkitage
here's where I'm stuck on verbage

Razzle stood and clapped with exuberance. "bravo, my dear Dazzle! The words drip from the page with the brilliance of a person who knows how to make the words drip from the page!"

Gustov replied "yes, I must agree! with gentle aroma the verbage swims across the imagination, designing a fumigated image of life that is as magnificus as a picture that smells really nice!”

[put something here that fills up this space]

Chapter 2

Dazzle said "your praises make me blush like a flower that has been planted in fertile mud with toy soldiers standing guard night and day, to ward off the dangers that lurk the forlorn pedals, weary from a heavy thunder shower that comes all of a sudden on an autumn's day."

"You should be flattered" said Razzle. "It was very very good and most pleasing. So much pleasing that I liked it very much."

"Yes," said Gustov. "I concur with the utmost of concurances" says Gustof while waiting for the pizza to finish warming in the toaster, scrounging around in the kitchen junk drawer, or as Dazzle says "je regarde dans le tiroir". while looking for an old name tag, Gustov realized there was no more aluminum foil.

Book 3

Gustof likes to use the toaster, especially when they are out of aluminum foil for head protection.

While he was playing in the drawer, he saw a strange key that he did not have labeled.

Gustov picked up the key and said “look, I found a key without label.”

“What do you think it belongs to?” said Razzle.

Gustov said “I don’t know. if I knew, it would have a label on it, because you know I always put labels on things so we can keep them straight, because a lot of our keys look alike, and we don’t know what will happen if we put the wrong key in the wrong spot, or the right key in the wrong spot, or the left key in the wrong spot, because we don’t know where we left it, because if we knew where we left it, we would have it on the schematics for the house, and then we would know where the key would go, and I would have putted a label on it."

Dazzle said, "an even more important question would be, 'whose key is it?' what if it isn't ours, and one of our friends who live near us left it in our drawers for storage so they wouldn't lose it?"

Razzle said "well, if they left it here, they should have put a label on it so we would know who it belongs to."

"unless," Dazzle interjected, "they didn't want us to know who it belongs to."

"or, " interjected Gustov they don't know what it belongs to."

"or, "interjected Razzle, "it might be both. They might not want us to know who it belongs to AND what it belongs to."

"Are you going to finish your piece of pizza?" Gustov said.

“who are you talking to?” said Dazzle.

“Well, being that Razzle is the only one with pizza left, I was targeting my comment towards him” said GUstov.

“I am actually not a fan of Pineapple,” responded Razzle. I was only eating it so i wouldn’t hurt your feelings. but if you would like it, you may have it.”

“That is so polite and thoughtful of you!” said Gustov. “I had no idea you were such a kind individual!”

Dazzle interjected, “J'aime le fromage sur mon calmar sandwich au beurre d'arachide.”

While finishing the last pizza, Gustov realize there was something hard in the pizza. Gustov pulled out a ring with an inscription on it that appeared mysterious and fascinating. On it was written the words:

ตุ่นปากเป็ดชอบที่จะเต้นบนสายลม.

Razzle said "if this inscription is right, the key Gustov found belongs to the ancient mountain squids who are trapped in a distant dimension guarded by a giant mountain eye and can only be freed if we find the mystic koockies of Woobagone and dip them in the everlasting fountain of milqshayke.

While spinning around, playing with remote control helicopter, Dazzle lost control, and the helicopter flew into an old picture of a random stranger that was left on the wall when Razzle, Dazzle, and Gustov moved into their flat. The picture fell down, and behind it was a key hole.

Gustove said "I wonder what key opens that key hole."

Razzle said "why don't you try the key you found in the refrigerator, Dazzle?"

So Dazzle took over the key and stuck it in the key hole on the wall. All of a sudden, the picture next to it - also with a random stranger left up when the previous owners disappeared - fell off the wall. There, on the wall, was a piece of paper.

"what is it?" said Gustov.

"I don't know!" said Razzle.

"Maybe we should check it out!" said Razzle.

Dazzle pulled it down. “It is written in an ancient Ugaric language!”

“Can you read it?” said Razzle.

“I will try!” said Dazzle.

“You are so smart!” said Gustov.

“Yes,” said Razzle. “We have no clue what we would ever do if you weren’t with us!”

“why thank you!” said Dazzle. “My ancient ugaritic is rusty but I will give it my best!”

“We know you can do it!” said Razzle.

“Yes!” said Gustov. “You are the best interpreter in the world! You have 100s of books on Amazon you have published yourself on the art of interpreting ancient languages! If there is anyone who can do it, it is you!”

Dazzle picked up the piece of paper and started to read.

Book 3

"Your interdimensional squid beat my interdimensional squid,
In a game of full contact badminton
It wasn't hard,
My squid is dead

Oh poor squid,
How I loved you
You were my play toy,
When I was young

I would bang you against
The metal railing on the staircase
And laugh with the heartiest of all laughes,
As you made funny faces with your eyebrows."

"Deep and cryptic!" said Razzle. "I wonder what it means!"

"Yes!" said Gustov. "It sounds mysterious!"

"But wait! THere is more!" said Dazzle.

"Then please continue!" said Gustov.

“Yes, please continue!” said Razzle.

“Then, continue I shall!” said Dazzle.

I and my squid went to Belgium,
To play a game of ping pong
It was a Tuesday,
And egg rolls were on sale

My Squid still lost
because it is still dead
and because I left my good racket at home
underneath the kitchen sink

And so they dragged me down,
To the misty side of a dream
And said don’t worry,
The carnival doesn’t start till 2:04

They said “we are all the squid,
So taste the egg rolls
And pour yourself a cup of tea,
For broken tiles cannot be changed while you
are standing on them

Book 3

So I put the pieces of life together,

And stared into the compact to straighten up my makeup

And made a resolution to never eat an egg roll

On Tuesday,

Because egg rolls are cheaper on Easter

and because squids apparently don't like fried tomatoes,

and neither do I

"So the secret must be in the tea cabinet!" said Gustov.

everybody ran to the tea cabinet. when they get there, they open the door, only to find a big mess.

JJ

Ch apter 5

"It looks like someone has been here already!" said Gustov.

"it looks like someone forgot to straighten up after making their tea last night!" said Razzle.

"It looks like someone had tea with their crumpets and didn't invite me!" weeped Dazzle bitterly.

"That is so cold!" said Gustov.

"Who would be so impolite to do such a thing!" said Razzle. "That's almost as unconsiderate as having tea but not inviting you, or having crumpets and not inviting you. but it's both crumpets AND tea! just so uncouth!"

Right then and there a ghoul in the shape of a

Right then and there a ghoul in the shape of a squid appeared, and it was wearing Gustov's favorite pair of lederhosen.

Before Gustov had a chance to get upset, the ghoul said "I needed something to wear. it is really cold in your closet at night."

Gustov let down his guard. "yes, I guess I keep the closet at a rather cold temperature. I keep it at a low temperature as a means of climate control. I don't actually have anything I need to keep at a cold temperature, but I do so just in case I find something that is best stored in a climate controlled environment."

"how very wise of you!" said Razzle.

"yes! very proactive!" said Dazzle.

"I have many items at home where that would be useful." said Julius Varny, the Squid Ghoul from the planet Meno.

"what kinds of things would that be?" said Gustov?"

"Why," said Julius, "I am so glad you ask. I have several collector comics that I fear are starting to be affected by my dimensions humidity level."

"Maybe we can have one shipped to your house. I hear InterdimensionalBay has a new interdimensional delivery system," said Razzle.

"That would be awesome!" said Julius. "Do you think they take PayInterdimensionalPal?"

"I would think so," said Dazzle.

"My 3 hearts melt with joy over the thought of having my very own climate control comic book cooler, or as we could call it, a 3CBC. To show my appreciation, I would like to share my glub glub zubber nub lub - or as you would call it - spam meatloaf," said Julius.

"while I appreciate your gratitude," said Dazzle, "I would not eat your glub glub with a spoon, I

would not eat it on the moon."

"I concur," said Razzle. "I would not eat it with a squid, I would not eat it in Madrid."

"I find myself agreement with my friends," said Gustov. "I would not eat them with a ghoul. I would not eat them at my school."

"I would not eat them in outer space! I would not eat it with hollandaise!" said Dazzle.

"I would not eat them with a ghoul squid! I would not eat them with a gold wig." said Razzle.

"I would not eat it with an orange! I would not eat it with a platypus!" said Gustov

"well, if you will not eat them in any way, then let me take you to the place I like to stay." said Julius.

On that, Julius took the key and stuck it in a hidden key hole above the radiator. The mirror turned into an intergalactic portal which sucked up Razzle, Dazzle, Gustov, and Julius.

“weeeee” said Dazzle.

“Wooooaaah” said Razzle

“Giddyup! Lets ride this horticultural oil for spider mites!” said Gustov.

“where are we going?” said Dazzle?

“I have no clue!” said Razzle.

“It could be anywhere!” said Gustov.

“Maybe even the center of the Galaxy!” said Razzle.

“Maybe even the center of the universe!” said Dazzle.

“Maybe even the center of the Milky Way!” said Gustov.

“actually, we are going to my house!” said Julius. “there we have egg rolls and tea. then after, there is a badmitten/ping/pong single round elimination match."

"Awesome!" said Razzle.

"What is the prize?" said Dazzle.

"I love prizes!" said Gustov.

"Well," said Julius. "if we win, then we will save the planet from imminent destruction. In my dimension, the physics derived from playing ping pong has the power to stop a large Anti-matter meteor from hitting the planet."

"What if we don't really know how to play?" said Dazzle.

"That's alright!" said Razzle. "it is not winning or losing that counts, but the restless energy released by the mighty power of your swing! so swing away! swing away all!"

So, after a brief trip to Julius' condo to feed the ghoul dogs, the quintet headed off to the tournament, but their spaceship was hindered by some intergalactic road construction. so while they waited for the construction crews to patch up the pot-holes in the space/time continuum, Dazzle said "while we wait, would you all like to hear a poem I have been working on?"

Razzle said "absolutely, Dazzle! Entertain us with your insightful prose that we so adore!"

Chapter 6

Gustov said “oooooh! another poem!”

and Julius said “what is this ‘poem’ thing that you are discussing?”

Dazzle said “It is where you open up your heart and let the heart flow onto the paper in poetic form!

“Poems are what make up poetry!” said Gustov.

“Yes! Poems are the poetry poets speak when they open up their heart and let the words flow! Dazzle is the master of all masters!”

Chapter 6

"Ah, yes!" said Julius. "we have those on my planet. We call them faniblabisakiwas!"

"Well, " said Dazzle. "this faniblabisakiwas is written in the Limitosis tri-language, spoken by the Limitosis people of the planet Ottowahni-kansas. This is about how I felt when I lost my first tooth.

"Dibble wah wah Gnopis
Dibble dibble wah gnopis
Dibble dibble dibble dibble
gnopsis dibble gnopsis dibble

Gnopsis dibble Gnopsis dibble
Gnopsis Gnopsis dibble
Wah Gnopsis dibble
Wah Dibble Gnopsis dibble

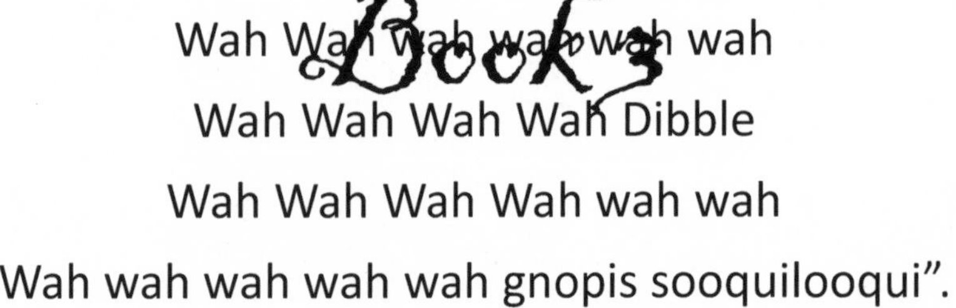

Wah Wah wah wah wah wah
Wah Wah Wah Wah Dibble
Wah Wah Wah Wah wah wah
Wah wah wah wah wah gnopis sooquilooqui”.

“Interesting,” said Razzle. “I take it that the Limitosis tri-language has only four words?”

“Well, they only had three,” said Dazzle, “up until a few days ago when they added a new one. The governing council met and voted unanimously to include a fourth word. there are still two additional words on the docket, and they will vote on them once someone figures out how to pronounce them.”

After a few hours, Julius said “this is taking forever! I am going to detour this puppy through a worm hole only a few of us elite drivers know about!” And on that note, Julius turned left and headed west. When they got to the portal, there was a sign that said:

“Zivil wivil waka woo”

"Oh no!" said Julius. "Apparently the portal is closed because the key to open it was lost 3 eons ago, and no one has been able to find it, so it is still lost, unless someone did find it but didn't know they found it, or they found it and are hiding it!"

Everybody pondered for a moment. Then Gustov said "Hey! Maybe the key I found in the drawer would work! It didn't have a label on it, so who knows what it might work on!"

"Didn't we use it for the portal at the house?" said Razzle.

"Well, yes!" said Dazzle. "But that doesn't mean it hasn't been fitted to work on more than one portal!"

"Why don't you get out and try it!" said Julius.

"Well, I forgot my space suit at home!" said Gustov.

"That's alright!" said Julies. "I can do it since I

am a ghoul and ghouls don't need space helmets."

"Thanks!" said Gustove as Julius took the key.

Julius went out the door towards to portal. but right before Julius was able to put the key in the portal, a meteor flew by and hit Julius, flinging Julius a million light years miles away.

"Oh well." said Dazzle. "I guess now we will never know."

"I guess we shant" said Razzle.

"Do you think Julius will be O.K.?" said Gustov.

"I am sure Julius will be O.k. Julius is a ghoul, and ghouls are immortal. but it will take Julius a while to get back, and by then we will be really old." said Dazzle.

pilogue

so with that, the three friends went home. It was dinner time, and they needed to get some sleep before work the next day.

The End

Book 3

[put something here that fills up this space]

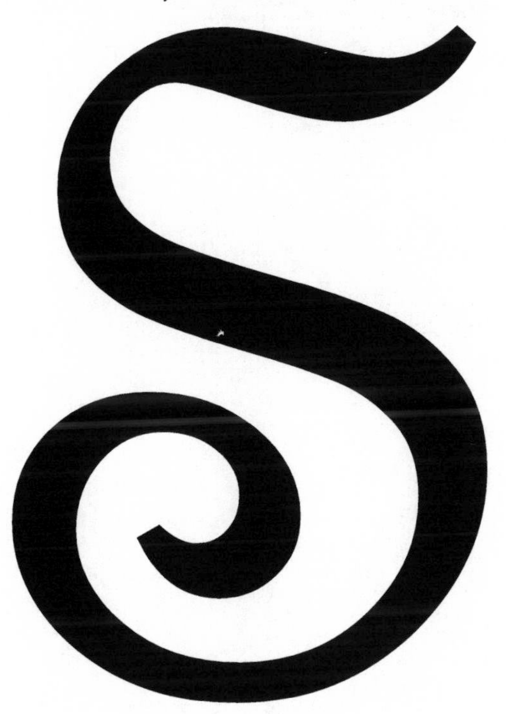

tay

tuned

Until the next exciting adventure!!!!

The Trilogy Continues!

azzle, Dazzle, and Gustov in the Court of Emporai Bufant

The trilogy continues...

By

Arsidious The Great

Five hundred twenty-sixth

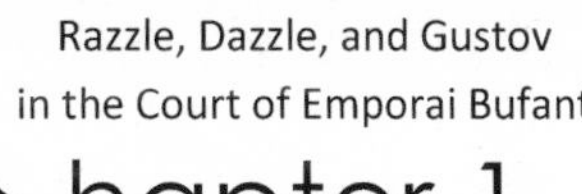

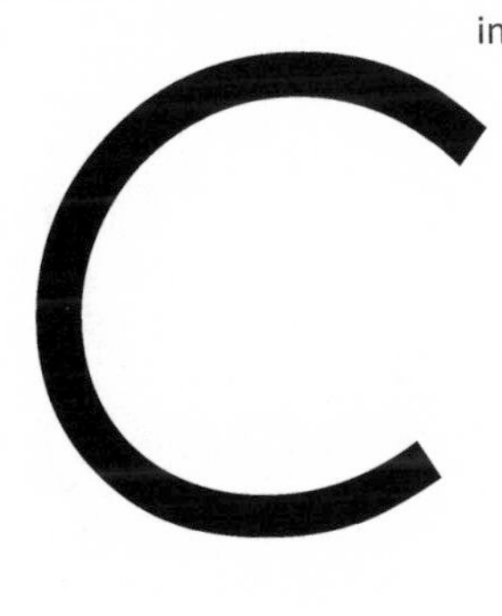

Chapter 1

"And so ends the tale of the Great Emporai Bufant's court of Lancers and Pokers of the Square Table!" Said Gustove.

"Excellent!" said Razzle.

"Yes!" Said Dazzle, "Yet I am still confused on the differences of Lancers and Pokers."

"Lancers, " said Gustov, "poke with lancers, while pokers lance with pokers."

"Ah!" Said Dazzle. "muchas gracias, my dear Gustov, for finally clearing that up for me.

"It is always my pleasure to enlighten my dear travelers with knowledge I have garnished through my many travels hither and fro, here and there, to and back again, over and over again as I travail the seven ponds and 11 land masses!"

"We always appreciate you endearing

us with your capricious knowledge and overflowing wisdom and insight." sentimented Razzle.

Yes" said Dazzle, "or as the French say, "mi burro es amarillo y tiene un horrible dolor de cabeza."

"It is knowledge like this that I have bestowed upon thee", reckoned Gustov, "that makes us wiser and empowers us to the task at hand!"

"And what task is that?" said Razzle.

"Yes, please tell!" said Dazzle. "We await to hear of the journey that waits before us!"

"Today", Gustov said with an air of majesty. "We are going to journey to the museum. For in the museum was found a note of all notes summoning all wise people to seek the door that would save Bufant's court and restore order to the land!"

"But wasn't the great court of Emporai Bufant hundreds of centuries ago, and in the distant country of Nashvilluta?" said Razzle.

"Yes, it was," said Dazzle. "Or at least I think that is what Gustove said," Dazzle said, finishing a cheese croissant, or as Dazzle called it, the Bizcocho de queso esponjoso.

"It was wiped out during the great crunchy woven wheat cracker shortage 200 years ago. When they ran out of their crunchy woven wheat cracker, they had nothing to eat their cheese wiz on, and the cheese wiz blew up one hot morning and destroyed the kingdom. The note said that the museums contained a magical door created by some trolls who built it so that people in the future could come and save their land by providing some new woven wheat crackers so they could use on the remaining cheese."

"This reminds me of a poem I wrote ," Said Dazzle.

"Let's hear it", said Gustov.

"Yes!" said Razzle.

"Horty torty,
william and gordy
Jumped the train,
even though they were 40

All they could do
was play every sporty
And josh away, josh
away all, till the pickles over ferment and
don't task like pickles any more.

So they packed up their stuff and left the grocery store and got on the trolley to head back to the flat so they could put up their lunch leftovers in their new refrigerator they were all so very proud of.

"Indubitably this is going to turn out to be the most exciting day ever!" yelled Razzle.

"I CAN HARDLY WAIT FOR ANOTHER MI-

NUTE!" shouted Dazzle. "IT"S LIKE THE MINUTES ARE GOING TRICKLY WICKLY DOWN A GIANT CLOCK SET ON A MOMENTOUS MOUNTAIN CALLED SIXTY SECOND MOUNTAIN!"

"I think my sandwich would have been better if I had the spicy brown mustard!" Screams Gustov.

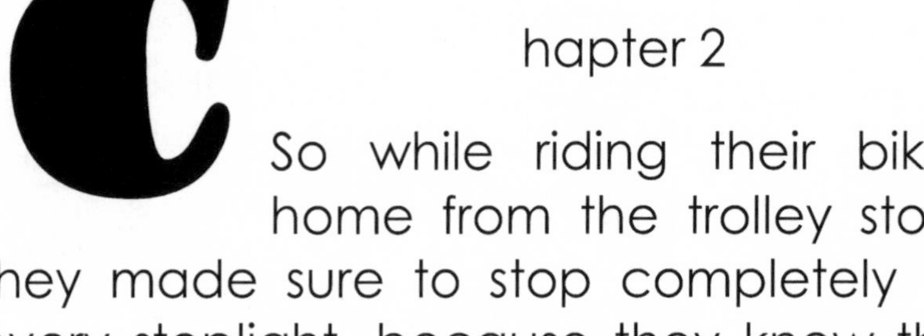

hapter 2

So while riding their bikes home from the trolley stop, they made sure to stop completely at every stoplight, because they knew the importance of being safe drivers. At the last stop, Dazzle said "did anyone see that tree on the right move?"

"No! " said Razzle.

"I did not either!" said Gustov.

"Maybe it was just my *mafaufau valea playing tricks on me again." said Dazzle.*

"Or," said Razzle all of a sudden. "Maybe it was that wizard hiding behind the pole I just saw peaking out!"

Everybody turned to look.

"Thee hast tasted the winter wind, and thee knowest the bitterest season of yesterday's rummage sale." said the wizard from the pole.

"He must be the ancient wizard we are looking for who knows the way to the Court of Bufant that was mentioned in your note!" said Gustov. "Let's follow the wizard!" said Razzle.

But before they could park their bikes, a horde of yellow llamas came running out of an alley.

"Oh NO!" said Dazzle. "The yellow llamas of the 7th realm! Flee!"

"They have fleas?" said Razzle.

"No, you silly Razzle. I mean take to flight as fast as you can! If their dribble gets on your bike, it will ruin the paint job!"

"OH NO!" said Gustov. "I work so hard to keep my bike's paint looking so pristine like I just bought it from the bike store last month!"

So the daring trio sped off as fast as they could, narrowly escaping the horde of yellow, paint messing, llamas.

"They have gone back! "Said Dazzle. "And not a moment too soon. My legs were getting tired."

"Mine too." said Razzle. "I tried to stretch them this morning, but I had no idea I would have to flee amarilla llamas!"

"I am glad I checked my tire pressure this morning!" said Gustov. "It was a little low, but I added more. I accidentally added too much, so I had to let a little out. I let out too much, but then, eventually I got it exact."

"It is important to have properly aired tires," said Razzle.

"Yes, said Dazzle. "One never knows when you will have to flee a horde of yellow llamas. It reminds me of a poem I wrote about butter substitute."

"Ooooh!" said Razzle. "I love a good spread on toast! Please let us hear it!"

"Yes, said Gustov. "Please endear us with your elucent soliloquy about butter that is not butter!"

Butter,
yet not butter
Spread,
but not bitter

Lather,
but not from an udder
It tastes like butter,
but it's not really

So much toast
for the lactose intolerant
A desire to savor
next to the fire hydrant

But it tastes so good
you could feed it to an ant
This substitute for jelly
It won't leave a scant

Everybody stood to their feet and claped as Dazzle took a bow.

"So illustrious!" said Razzle.

"Yes, so invigorating! I needed that after the flight from the angry yellow llamas." said Gustov.

hapter 3

So everyone parked their bike, took off their helmet, and made sure to lock them up tight so as to not tempt any passer-by strangers. Then Dazzle said "Do you think we should disengage the front wheel as well? I heard that it can be used as an additional deterrent to people who might accidentally take the wrong bike home."

"That is a most excellent idea!" said Razzle.

So Gustov pulled out a wrench from the tool belt Gustov wears under the coat and disengaged everyone's wheel.

"There we go, dizzy doh" said Gustov. "Now everyone's bike will be safe!"

"Awesome sauce!" said Razzle!

"Thanks a million, Gustov, the great tire disengager!" said Dazzle.

"No problemo, my dearest comraderies!" said Gustov. "Now let's go catch that wizard!"

"So which way did the wizard do si do?" said Razzle.

"I think the wizard zizzard do-si-doed right into our fabuolos library!" replied Gustov.

"Awesome sausages!" said Dazzle smiling. "Let us take into pursuit this mysterious wizard until answers are bequeathed to us the purpose of the wizard's appearance in our world!"

So the daring trio gathered their belongings and headed into the library.

As they passed the front desk, Razzle said "hey, I need to stop by the snazzy lazzy front desk and see if I can have them reserve a copy of the latest edition of the Bob Ross autobiography? I am the biggest fan, and the Bob Ross autobiography inspires me to greatness every time I read it. And if it is being updated with new pages, I must get it so I can be the first one inspired by its greatness!"

"Sure, Razzle!" said Dazzle. "That shouldn't be an issue. If it were an issue, I surely would have issued an issue on the issue."

"Reserve-a-derv-away!" said Gustov. "One should never let an opportunity like that pass by without at least the attempt to reserve."

So Razzle went to the front desk. Then they heard Razzle scream "YES! I HAVE IT!"

"I think Razzle got it." said Dazzle to Gustov.

"I hope so!" said Gustov to Dazzle. "Razzle has been expecting this for a long time."

Chapter 5

Razzle came back so happy to have gotten the book on reserve.

"Let us continue our hunt for the mysterious wizard!" said Gustov.

So the trio looked around.

"There the wizard is!" said Dazzle. "The wizard is behind the formica bush!"

So the trio headed to the formica bush, only to find it was an old prop for some movie with Trolls and Elves.

"Where could the wizard have gone to?" said Razzle.

"Why don't we check the section with wizards and stuff?" said Dazzle.

"Sounds like an idea! " said Gustov.

"Sounds like a rootin tootin great idea!" said Razzle.

So the trio ran to the section of the library with wizards. But the wizard was not there.

"Oh shanana bananas!" said Gustov. "I was so sure the wizard would be here."

"Me too!" said Razzle.

"I as well!" said Dazzle.

The trio pondered. Then Razzle's eyes started to be sparkelishish.

"Maybe the wizard went to the cooking section! After doing all that time-traveling, I am sure the wizard might be hungry!"

"Why that is so insightful!" said Gustov.

"Yes! So brilliantly insightful into the soul of an individual who has traveled through time to arrive right here in our time. It's like an insight into the mind who is insightful!"

So they blazed over to the cooking section like people in a rush to get something somewhere. As they got closer, they heard chanting.

"Ohm nom chiver mi timbers

Sloppy noppy middle of decembers

A tissle a tassle a plate of gimbers

Limpy lompy lampy limbers.

"It's like fitting berries in the blender, " said Razzle.

"I like berry smoothies," said Gustov.

"Do you think they have smoothies in the Court of Bufant?" said Dazzle.

All of a sudden, Chizzle the great wizard of the Court of Bufant appeared before the trio. "Didst thee hearest thou mentioneth ze sacredness of ze Courts of the Great Bufant?"

"Why, yes, dearest Chizzlie! We receiveth thou ancient note which echoeth thy cry for helps." said Razzle.

"Yes," said Dazzle, "we were behoved by the passion of thy cry inscribed on thy duilleagan seòlta to seaketh out thy face that we mightest partake of the solution to saveth the great and glorious kingdome that is the Court of Bufant."

"So, if thou wilst, lead us on, dear Chizzlery!" said Gustov.

"Come, my chivalrous Chardinaire of chivary." said Chizzle.

As they started to head off, a band of purple marmosets jumped out of the drain and started running towards the trio.

"Oh no!" cried Razzle. "Purple marmosets from the 8th dimension! Don't let them touch you or you will instantly get a nasty leg cramp!"

"Oh no!" cried Dazzle." "Not a leg cramp!"

"I hate leg cramps!" cried Gustov. "They are almost as bad as arm cramps but they happen in your leg instead!"

Everyone started to dash to and fro, from hither to tither, till they lost all the marmosets.

"The Marmosets must have gotten tired and returned to the 8th dimention to rest back up for their next attack." said Chizzle in an ancient accent.

Chizzle lead the trio to the elevator that had been taped off.

"This elevator werst yonder in this place here longeth prior to the building. And yon elevator has never been in working condition. The Tape of non-operation hast garnish this since the dawn of the construction." said Razzle.

Chapter 6

"Is this the secret portal machine that is disguised as an elevator?" saidith Dazzle.

"I have never donned through the gates of an ele-portal!" Said Gustov.

"Take grappings of thy garments!" said Chizzle.

Chizzle pressed the second floor. It rolled to the second floor, which popped open to the cafeteria.

"Are we there yet?" said Dazzle.

"No, I was just thirsty," said Chizzle. "Anyone one for a fluffy soda?"

"No thanks." said Razzle. "I appologizeth, but We shan't be willing to take drinks from strangers."

Chapter 7

"I was just testing thee," said Chizzle. "It appears thou wisdom and chivary art great and thou art worthy to take on the task ahead! For even though I taunted you and teased you and tested thee with the sweetest of all necters, thou resisted and stood by thou principles!"

"Thank you, most honorable of all wizards. Now lead us to the Court of Boufant that we shalst save the land from its imminent demise." said Razzle.

"But how shaleth we travel to the fushat e purpurta?" said Dazzle

"Enter back into the vertical carriage!" said Chizzle.

Everyone entered back in.

"So now what?" said Gustov.

"Enter the magic combination!" said Chizzle.

“What art the magic combination?” said Razzle.

“Well, I don’t remember it,” said Chizzle. “If I knew the answer,” said Chizzle, “I would have used it to go home.”

“Ok” said Dazzle. “I guess it’s up to us to figure it out. While we think, I have a poem I can read.”

Lopsided lollipops
line the land
Where goose and gander
trollup and stand

Upon the valley,
the Hubbababa land
Waiting for the truck
to deliver a kick stand

For the Mice and the
musicians are all ready to play
As the wicker chairs and
velvet stairs show us the way

To a brighter window
where the glare gives us stay
And down will come fluffy

pillows, we all scream Yeah!

For Night is a whisper,
Time is a harness
We will echo the distance
in all of it's fairness

For hair nets and chair rails
hold stay in the wilderness
There are children in line,
waiting to play chess

"Excellent, dear friend!" said Chizzle. "Words so swooning have nary brushed mine ears all these many years. I await to hear more of thy most excellent prose!!"

"Dazzle is our resident scribe, for from Dazzle's pen flow words of inspiration and opulence!" said Razzle.

"Yes!" said Gustov. "Without Dazzles wit and rhyme, there wouldst be many a day we would be found lost in yonder wilderness."

Gustov said "I'm hungry. I thinkst I shallst

have a snacketh." So Gustov pulls out a fortuneate cooking from the back pack. While chewing on the cookie, Gustov realized the fortunate words were still in the cookie. Dazzle pulled it out of Gustov's mouth and took a look at it.

"It is an ancient codex!" said Dazzle. "But how will we ever decipher the numbers?"

"Wait" said Gustov. "I remember this. It's from an ancient book of riddles we used to have in the pantry. We have to take each number, divide by 17 and then multiply the number by the remainder. We then roundeth yon number to the nearest 13th and then split the difference with a song about blueberries!"

"So punch in the numbers already!" said Razzle.

So, as Razzle started to type in the numers, a cloud of purple marmosets riding yellow llamas came charging out of the World History section.

"QUICK!" said Dazzle.

"YES QUICK! THey are carrying hand-books full of government mandates from various regimes!"

"If we don't hurry," said Chizzle, "we are going to have to hear them recite awful codex Memorandi On Business Casual Dress Policy

Razzle starting calculating faster than a person could normally calculate. Razzle pressed the button and the door close. As the door closed, they could hear the faint whispers of public policy being read out loud.

"That was so incredibly close!" said Dazzle.

"YES!" Said Gustov. "Last time I had to listen to public policy, my eyelashes fell out!"

"Thou meanest those aren't real?" said Chizzle.

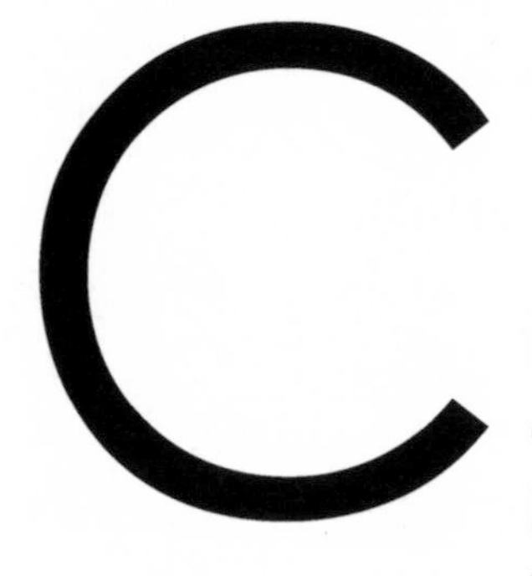

hapter 8

"Well, contrary to the belief of some, eyelashes do grow back, especially when they fell out during periods of duress," said Gustov "Public policy would definitely fit that definition," said Razzle.

"I once worked in a office where they had a book on public policy." said Dazzle.

So the trio flew back in time and space and to the Courts of the Emporai Bufant. When they arrived, a host of dignitaries awaited them. "We have waited long and even longer for thou arrival to our court! We send thou greetings from the Emporai who govern our land! Please follow us."

As they walked down the hall, they saw people holding purple marmosets and riding yellow llamas.

Gustov turned to the other two and said "I think this is a trap. On my say, let us escape from this treacherous land."

"Yes, I must concur." said Razzle. "I think it is a trap."

"I am starting to agree with you all as well." said Dazzle.

"Well, I think you might be right." said Chizzle. "I don't see my friend, Arvotamah, who usually leaves out a nice spread for interdimensional guests."

"Let's go!" said Gustov. And everyone ran for the entrance. As they turned to the west, they saw a court that looked almost exactly identical, except for a nice spread set out by Arvotamah, and of course, no purple marmosets or yellow llamas.

"This must be the right place," said Chizzle.

"Come hither on in" said Arvotamah. We hast been waiting for thou to arrivest."

“Thank you” said Razzle, bowing.

“Thank you,” Gustove said, jumping up and down (for that is how people great each other where Gustov is from).

“Txipiroi txakurkumeak,” said Dazzle spinning in circles.

“Codorna laranja,” said Chizzle, floating in the air.

The trio entered in to the courts, where they were greeted by the Emporai: Fintofeans, Feterfaloon, and Ix.

The Emporai turned and said “Hast thou brought the coveted woven biscuit of wheat?”

Dazzle said “nope.”

Razzle said “neither dost I.”

Gustov said “I think I left it on the table at the library,”

The Emporai sighed “oh me oh my, now we will all accidently blow up in a glorious explosion of canned cheese!”

"Isn't there any other way we can assist thee?" said Dazzle.

"Yes, there must be another way." said Razzle.

"Can we eat the cheese without the woven wheat treats? I am sort of hungry." said Gustov.

"Alas" said Chizzle. "The only other way is if a valaint trio of worth friend can pull out the stick stuck in the mud. For you see, it is jamming the door to the stash of crackers we keepeth in the doomsday vault."

"We can try!" said Razzle.

"Yes, we would be glad to try!" said Dazzle.

"We need to get a hurryin on. I am getting weak from lack of food." said Gustov.

"If we can get it open," said Chizzle, "there will be all the food your heart would desire. We have enough food for 1000 years in case a meteor strikes the earth and we have to stay in it until another earth forms."

On that note, Gustove went over to the stick and pulled and pulled and pulled and pulled and pulled and pulled. Suddenly, the stick pulled out and the doors flung open. Everybody cheered. Everybody started to celebrate, until they saw a giant dragon fly out.

"So THAT'S where Gragon the tiniest dragon went to!" said Chizzle.

"Apparently Gragon ate a lot while down there, because there is nothing left."

"Oh no!" said the Emporai. "What are we going to do? THe cheese will explode at any moment!

All of a sudden, Gragon went over to the cans of cheese and ate them all. Everyone went 'yeah! We are saved."

All of a sudden Gragon let a gigantic belch, and then Gragon exploded. But instead of blowing up into small dragon parts, Gragon blew up into a bunch of little dragons.

With everyone safe, the trio decided to head home. They said good-bye to each little dragon and to their new friends, Chizzle, the Emporai, the Yellow Llamas, and the purple marmosets.

They went back through the elevator, to the library, where Gustov grabbed the box of crackers and ate most of them, not noticing the little dragon that had hitched a ride on the back of Gustov's jacket...

he

nd

[leave this page
blank like they
do in all those
other books]

All the leaves are sleeping gently in the tree as the clouds set quietly on the mountain and the fish have all gone home

By Arsidious The Great Writer

ALL THLBOOK VJS ARSBOOK LOVB IN THTR ABOOK THCLOUDS ST QUITLY ON THBOOKE MOUNTAIN AN THBOOK FISH HAVE ALL GONE HOME

All the leaves are sleeping gently in the tree as the clouds set quietly on the mountain and the fish have all gone home.

Razzle and Dazzle and Gustov have traveled far and were tired from the many adventures their random occurrences have taken them.

Or were they random?

Was some intergalactic force of nature overlooking their every move, guiding each jilted step to the next, even more jilted step?

Have the binoculars of a traveler of the gilded stream of space traversed their destiny and superimposed it on to a fate not yet seen?

Razzle pondered this as the stars glistened in the abyss above the inquisitive Razzle's head. Dancing are the stars above, singing to the void as though a sentient wind blew above them. When all of a sudden, 7 green lima bean sized Darkansasans pierce the night wallet and hovered above the unsuspecting trio.

Ping ping ping go the Darkansasans phasers, bouncing off the trio as they gaze at the night sky. It appears as though nothing is happening. The trio does not even realize that the Darkansasans are pinging them with their phasers.

As the Darkanasans zip back into the night sky, Razzle says "Hey, did anyone notice the leaves on the trees and how they glisten in the moonlight?"

"No", expressed Dazzle. "But now that you mention it, the leaves are very beautiful tonight!"

"Yes," articulated Gustov, looking at the trees in wonder. "The leaves are speaking to us as though there is something important we are missing."

The trio looked in the sky. Razzle looked north. Dazzle looked East. Gustov looked South. Razzle looked West. Dazzle looked North. Gustov just walked around in circles.

As they looked up, they noticed that everything around them was growing bigger.

"Did you notice everything around us is getting bigger?" modulated Dazzle.

"Yes, I did notice that. Quite interesting." narrated Razzle.

"Actually, I wasn't paying attention," pronounced Gustov. "I was busy walking around in circles."

Growing, Growing, everything was growing.

"How is everything growing like that?" uttered Razzle.

"How much will it grow?" voiced Dazzle.

"When does everything stop spinning?" communicated Gustov.

Next thing they knew, a giant katydid came up to them.

"Hello, Mrs Katydid. How are you doing?" asked Razzle.

"How do you know it's a Mrs.?" inquired Dazzle.

"Well," vocalized Razzle, "it's called a Katy-did. Not a Kevin-did. Not a Karl-did."

"Sooo." pondered Gustov. "What do they call a boy Katydid?"

"Hmmmmmm" every body went.

Next thing, the Katydid bit the top off a dandelion.

"Hey, I don't think the katydid wants to talk. I think it wants to eat us!" described Razzle.

"What brought you to that conclusion?" appealed Dazzle.

"Well, it bit the top of the dandelion!" revealed Razzle.

"Yes, but how do we know if it is simply hungry for vegetables and not carnivorous." proclaimed Gustov.

"Well, maybe you can look it up on your phone," reported Razzle.

"That's a great idea!" reckoned Dazzle.

Razzle, Dazzle, and Gustov pulled out their phones. Gustov realized the phone he had would not work because it was just a flip phone.

"Well, the good news is they mostly eat vegetation." suppositioned Razzle.

“That is very good news.” held Dazzle.

“What it is the bad news?” requisitioned Gustov.

“THey also like small animals.” recounted Razzle.

“Oh.” considered Dazzle. “That could be very bad news.”

The katydid’s head started looking down at the trio, who were now the size of ants.

“I guess we should run!” divulged Razzle.

On that, the trio ran. They ran and they ran. Up the hills and down the hills, through the grass, around the rocks. They traversed the puddles, and jumped the cracks in the ground. They dodged ants and other creepy crawlies. They would rest against leaves and try not to touch the icky slugs.

While running, they saw a hole in the ground.

Chapter 2

"Jump!" Razzle verified.

They all jumped into the hole and waited for the katydid to pass. They waited and waited and waited. Then Dazzle poked his head up and looked around.

"Humm, apparently the katydid didn't chase us." Dazzle said.

After crawling out of the hole, they saw 3 space ships that was just their size.

“Cool!” said Gustov. “I always wanted to drive a space ship!”

“Me too!” said Razzle!

“I as well would like to drive a spaceship. I remember Tabitha talking about them in class.” said Dazzle.

Everybody jumped into their spaceship and took off.

“I am going to call mine Zippy,” said Razzle.

“I am going to call mine Happy Trails,” said Dazzle.

"I am going to call mine Bing-Bang-Kanichy-wee-wah" said Gustov.

"I am going to call mine Charles," narrated Penelope.

"You named your car Charles!" said Razzle. "How are you going to tell them apart?" Razzle revealed over the deeply intricate communication device.

"I just called my car 'Carl'. I changed it yesterday as I was cleaning the interior. I thought it reminded me more of a Carl than a Charles." said Penelope.

"I would agree," said Razzle. "I really thought Charles was sort of an off fit for your car. Carl is a much better choice." "Why, thank you, Razzle!" Penelope, pulling ahead over everyone else.

"Follow me!" said Penelope. "I think I know the way out of here!"

So everyone formed a straight line behind Penelope as they zoomed past leaves, branches, giant moths, and the occasional yield sign.

“Shouldn’t we slow down when we approach those yield signs?” said Dazzle.

“Well, they are yields and not stop signs” said Gustov. “I mean, technically we should, but the likelihood of us coming to those signs at the same time as another spaceship is small.”

“But it still could happen!” said Dazzle.

“I guess you are right!” said Razzle.

So at the next yield sign, everybody slowed down to a safe speed. Then they zoomed off again, following Penelope into the clouds.

On the way up to the clouds, they saw a couple of lost balloons.

“Oh man, I miss my balloon” said Dazzle. “It reminds me of a poem I wrote about it. Would you like me to share it?”

“Please do!” said Razzle.

"Oh, yes! I love your poems!" said Gustov.

"You write poems?" inquired Penelope. "I would love to hear one of your poems!"

"O.K." said Dazzle. "Here it goes!"

Oh Balloon
You left too soon
Like a baboon
Who fell in love with a spoon

You took to the sky
I will never understand why
It made me cry
Oh why oh why oh why

I waited for you to return
Page after page I would turn
Only to learn
That forever I would yearn

For you never would come back
Even though I would stack
Your favorite stack

On the back of my back pack

I figure you just found another
To treat you like a feather
On the breath of the distant weather
Going where other balloons wouldst gather.

I wait until the day
I will see you come my way
And we can go and play
Among the aquifoliaceae

For a moment in time, the world stopped.

"That was the most beautiful thing I have ever heard!" Penelope said, wiping the tears away.

"Yes, I concur," said Razzle. "My innermost being was stirred to the utter most!"

"I will never stop weeping these tears of grieving!" said Gustov.

Chapter 3

"Thank you so much, my friends!" said Dazzle. "Your encouragement lifts me above the clouds!"

"Speaking of clouds," said Razzle, "I think we are above them now!"

Everybody looked.

“Wow!” said Gustov.

“Oh my goodness!” said Dazzle.

“Gosh oh gracious!” said Razzle.

“Yes! We made it!” said Penelope.

All of a sudden, a giant vaccuum tube came out of nowhere and started sucking all the air up into it.

“Oh no!” said Razzle.

“Golly Gee” said Dazzle.

“I just spilt my mocha!” said Gustov.

“Where did that come from?” said Penelope.

“That reminds me, I forgot to clean up where I dropped the flower all over the floor." said Dazzle.

"Everybody, turn the opposite way and hit the gas! We have to escape the vacuum!" said Razzle.

Everybody turned and hit the gas as hard as they could. Unfortunately, they could not-out pull the incredible vacuum. They found themselves being pulled up a vacuum tube into a large intergalactic Dyson vacuum. Sitting in the container where all the dust and stuff go in the vacuum, they wait.

"I hope they hurry up," said Dazzle. "I'm not sure, but I think there is some west indies goose down in here, and I am slightly allergic to west indies good down. "

"I have some allergy medicine in my pocket" said Penelope.

"Why thank you!" said Dazzle. "But no thank you. I try not to take medicine from others. I never know how it might react to something else I am taking."

"You are a very safe and smart individual!" said Penelope.

"I know! "Said Razzle. "Dazzle works very hard to be a good role model and practices safety constantly."

All of a sudden, a laser comes out of Gustov's ship.

"Hey, everybody! I reconfigured the guidance system to project a laser that we could us cut open the vacuum bag!" said Gustov.

"Awesome!" said Razzle.

"Yes! Absolutely ingenious!" said Dazzle.

"I knew if anyone could do it, it would be you!" said Penelope.

"O.K. everyone, just follow my lead and point the laser at the weak point of the vacuum bag. If it is like most vacuum bags, it is about 2 inches below the highest point. At our current size, I am calculating it as 17.34 feet from the top."

Everyone calibrated their lasers to hit 17.34 feet from the top and fired.

Gustov's laser was green.

Razzle's laser was blue.

Dazzle's laser was chartreuse.

Penelope's laser came out Periwinkle.

As the lasers combined, they became a glorious beam of cornflower blue. nothing.

"We need more power!" said Dazzle.

"Deviate power from the turbo thrusters!" said Razzle.

"OK!" said Gustov.

"Got it!" said Penelope.

As they increase the power, the light changed to a Veronese / Viridian. The vacuum case started to crackle.

“We need more power!” said Dazzle.

“Deviate power from the Helicon double-layer thrusters!” said Gustov.

“Yes! “Said Razzle.”

“If anything should do it, that will do it!” said Penelope.

As they increased the power again, the light changed to a Quinacridone magenta. The vacuum case started to smolder.

“MORE POWER!” said Gustov.

“Deviate power from the silicon-germanium thermoelectric Magnetorquer!" said Penelope.

"That should do it!" said Razzle.

"I am sure that will work!" said Dazzle.

"Awesome!" said Gustov.

As they increase the power, the laser changed to a Razzmic Berry. As the bag started to smoke, the zipper on the vacuum bag opened up, and a giant eye poked through the crack.

"Excuse me," said the giant voice. "Please stop. I just bought this vacuum, but it was used, so there was no warranty."

The group flew their ships out of the vacuum hole. On the other end, they saw a giant looking space alien. They gasped.

"A giant!" said Dazzle.

"No, Not really a giant. The alien is just really large because we were shrunk." said Razzle.

"Yes, " said the alien. "I needed to shrink you so I could suck you up in my vacuum cleaner."

"That is a brilliant plan!" said Razzle.

"I agree," said Dazzle."

I couldn't have thought of a better plan," said Gustov.

"Have you seen my notebook? " said Penelope. "I would love to take notes."

"You can borrow mine" said Gustov.

Everyone took a pause.

ALL THILBOOK VJS ARSBOOK LOVB INTHTR ABOOK THCLOUDSST QUITLY ONTHBOOKE MOUNTAIN AN THBOOK FISHHAVE ALL GONE HOME

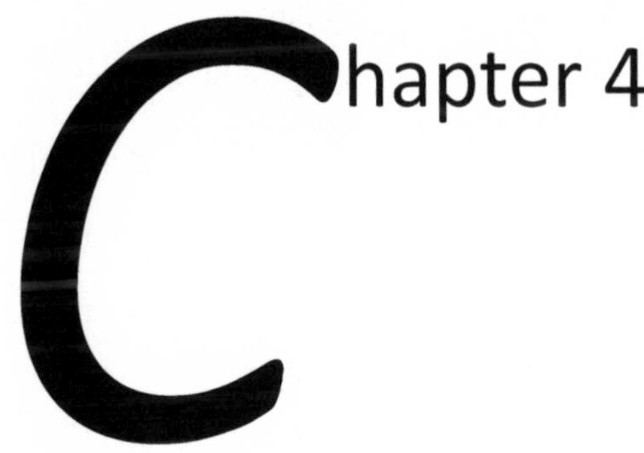

hapter 4

[write intricate chapter about how they met the exquisite oversear of all things and how the oversear explained all the great mysteries they came across that ties everything together]

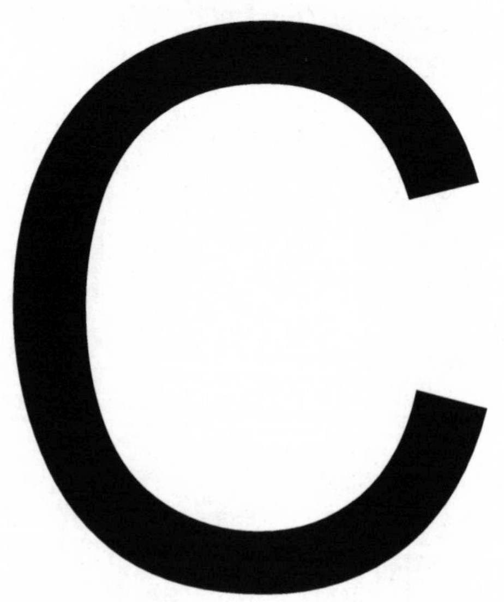

hapter 5

“I couldn’t have thought of a better plan,” said Gustov.

“Have you seen my notebook? “ said Penelope. “I would love to take notes.”

“You can borrow mine” said Gustov.

Everyone took a pause.

“So why did you bring us here?” said Dazzle.

“Yes, it really is a complicated move you pulled to get us here.” said Razzle.

“Actually, I enjoyed it so far.” said Gustov.

“I find it a really enjoyable adventure too,” said Penelope.

“Well,” said the alien. “I was sitting there, enjoying some freshly dethawed hummus, and this balloon came out of nowhere and got stuck in my window. I would pull it out, but I don’t have any fingers.”

“We can get it,” said Razzle.

“Yes, we would be glad to assist. Just show us where it is.” said Gustov.

So the alien pointed to where the balloon was sitting next to the window.

The alien said “I could have just opened the window, but I didn't know where it would go, and was worried it would fly away, knowing somebody out there lost it.”

“We understand,” said Dazzle. “Just point the direction.”

So the alien pointed up at the window. It was at that moment, Dazzle recognized the balloon lost so long ago.

“My balloon!” said Dazzle.

“We are so glad you found your balloon!” said Gustov.

“And just in time for dinner!” said Razzle.

“Well let's grab the balloon and head off

for home" said Penelope.

"Thank you so much!" said Cheswelda.

They grab the balloon. Cheswelda said "Thank you" as they headed out to go home.

"That was a great adventure!" said Dazzle.

"Yes it was," said Razzle.

"I loved it!" said Gustov.

"Well, I will see you all later!" said Penelope. "It is time for me to head back to feed my venus fly trap."

"Well, you better grow back the right size," said Dazzle. "The venus fly trap may try to eat you!."

Dazzle laughed.
Razzle Laughed.
Penelope
laughed.
Gustov laughed.
Cheselda laughed.
Terance laughed.
It was a great time.
It was the best time
ever.

Everybody agreed

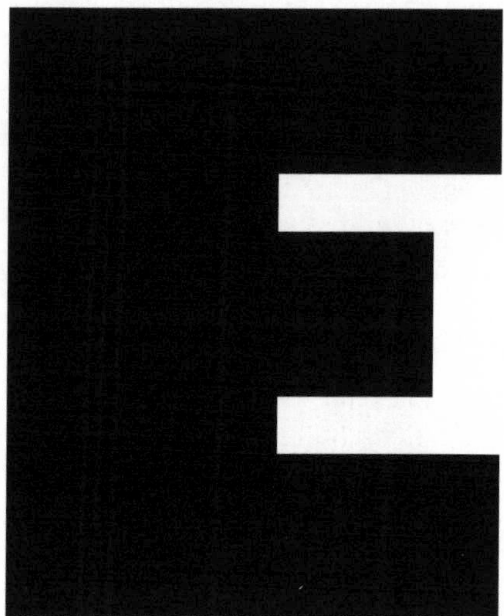

pilogue

Gustov laughed. Cheselda laughed. Terance laughed. It was a great time. It was the best time ever. Everybody agreed it was really fun, and they hoped to do it again really soon so they could

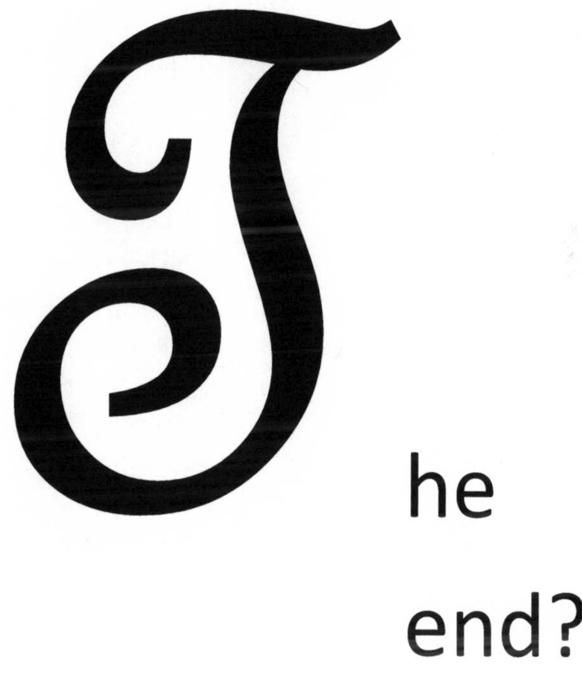

he

end?

141st

ALL THLBOOK VJS ARSBOOK LOVB IN THTR ABOOK THCLOUDS ST QUITLY ON THBOOKE MOUNTAIN AN THBOOK FISH HAVE ALL GONE HOME

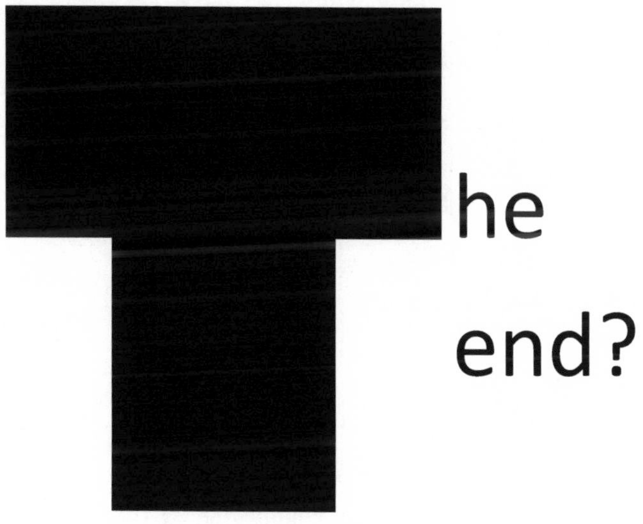

he

end?

I'm Razzle

By Arsidious The Great Writer

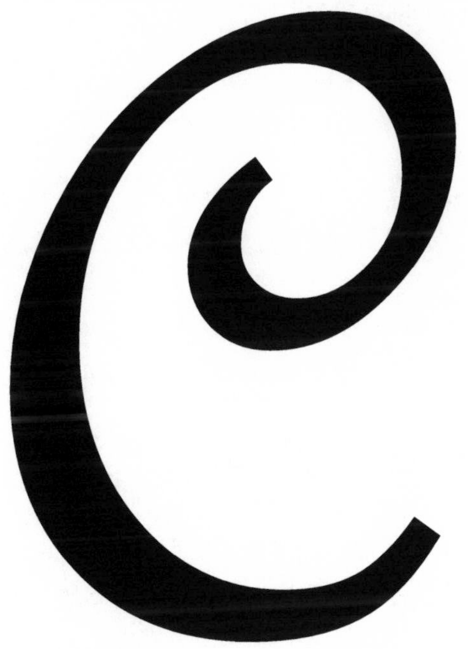

hapter 1

From the Wind and the rain I was born!

Of mighty powers that the universe could no longer contain.

I hold within me great secrets that I use in my travels to and fro.

Very few things have not rendered before mine eyes.

I literally have tasted great sorrows and tested great mountains.

The yearning of the waters hear my voice.

I am Razzle, friend to the rock and the iguana and the plastic pink flamingo bird (not to be confused with the plastic pink flamingo fish, which I utterly despise!)

I am the flower that grows in the marsh, waiting for the mighty alligator to pass, that I might devour it in my leaves.

I eat my potato chips on the park bench as the squirrels dash below my feet, waiting for just a morsel to fall!

Hillsides display my footprints, hardened in the mud, cooked by the blazing sun!

I like to literally dance in the rain!

I like to run through the meadows!

I like artificial cheese spread on crackers!

Take me away, Calgon!

I came to earth at a time when this planet needed a Razzle.

I am that Razzle.

Trouble echoed through the rain gutters.

If all I have done in my time here on this planet were laid up in a line, it would be a really long line.

A really really long line.

The line would be so long, I would have to travel far just to see the other end of the line.

If the line was straight, we might have to make a bridge, unless we decided that it would be alright to make the line perforated across land masses.

I arrived here on this planet on a rainy afternoon, when the flowers were taking in the morning waters.

I stopped at the local store to get a poncho so my alien attire would not get ruined by the heavenly pour, for even though my attire was made from the fibers of Gistobiwanki leaves from the planet Furbistankinawa, my attire was not properly treated to withstand all the heavenly pour.

After obtaining a beautiful plastic mono-color garb to protect my alien attire made from the fibers of Gistobiwanki leaves from the planet Furbistankinawa, I literally ventured out to discover what I could find on this planet from which I arrived.

The planet from which I came was Tetrahenious.

It was literally shaped like a tetrahedron, caused by the tetrahedronite that made up the crust of the planet.

Most of my friends came from Trapazodion and Hexagron.

We like to play a game we called Sliders and Climbers.

hapter 2

And eat cheese spread on crackers.

I left because I grew restless.

The Great Outer Reef of space called to me.

It said "Razzle, you need to go travel to the Great Outer Reef of space.

It's really great!

I am sure you will like it a lot.".

So I hopped into my space craft and headed for the Great Outside Reef.

My space craft was made from the best materials I could find from my travels.

Rods from the land of Rodulan, Reels from the land of Reeladulou, Steel from Steelisone, Wires from Wirito, Tires from Tironia, Gears from Gearundia, instruction manuals from Instructamanuala, and pens from Pensacola.

My intergalactic space craft was fueled with the juice from buzz buzz berries, because they had that buzz that made the intergalactic space ship go vrooom vrooom.

As I moved closer to the Not So Great Inner Reef (which I had to pass to get to the Greater Outer Reef - it's called that because it is so obviously so much greater and it is OUTSIDE, whereas the Not-So-Great one is meh, and it is INSIDE).

All of a sudden, a Great Outside Reef creature popped out of the Not so Great Reef and growled an awful growl.

I could not tell if it was stuck, or angry, or hungry, or angry because it was stuck, or stuck because it was angry and hungry.

So I stopped my intergalactic space vehicle, rolled down my window, and said "are you angry, stuck, or hungry because you are stuck and angry?"

[Discuss "the thing"]

The creature turned towards me and said with a growl: “I am angry because I am hungry because I have been stuck here for days, far away from my home in the Great Outerspace Reef..”

“Oh.

Ok.” I said as I now had my answer.

So I literally rolled up my window and continued on my journey, proud that I had actually figured out the answer before I asked.

But then again, I knew I would, because I am super insightful like that.

But as I neared the Greater Outsourced Reef, I saw a small, one eyed, Not So Great Inner reef, creature.

It looked like it was tangled up in the Great Otter Reef.

I surmised it got stuck when it lost its contacts just passing through and got stuck trying to find it.

I pulled over and said “what’s the matter, little space creature?”

The creature turned to me and said “oh, I could barely see you!

For you see, I have lost my spectacles, and now I cannot see a thing!”

That’s scary not to be able to see if

you lose your spectacles.

One moment you can see.

The next moment you cannot.

And you can't fix it, because the spectacles you would use to fix it are not where you think they are, because they are lost.

I was beside myself.

I was sure it would have been contacts.

But a spectacle was pretty impressive.

I would find it hard to lose my spectacles, because they are pretty large.

This creature must have either really small spectacles, or is as blind as a bat.

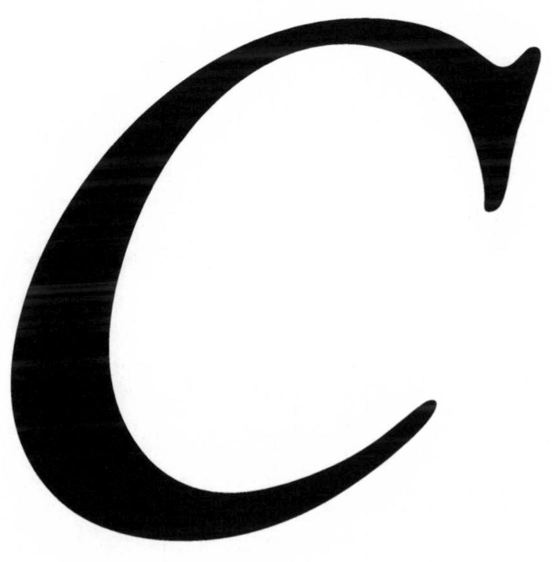

hapter 4

As I passed by the local intergalactic convenience store, I pulled in to grab a snack, because I was getting hungry in that I had been traveling for hours and then finding myself distracted by those various creatures who were so inconveniently stuck in opposing reefs.

Maybe they could call each other and switch places.

Then at least they would be in their own corresponding reefs.

I also pulled up to fill up my space craft.

But when I pulled up, their pumps said they were out of buzz buzz berry bonanza, which is what I really prefer in my space craft, because they had that buzz that made the intergalactic space ship go vrooom vrooom.

I went inside and asked them when the next shipment of buzz buzz berry banaza was going to get here because it had that buzz that made the intergalactic space ship go vrooom vrooom.

The attendant said that there was a shipment on the way, but the driver got stuck in the Not-So-Great inner reef several days ago, and no one was able to get the driver out.

THey even sent a tow truck space ship that way, but apparently the driver lost the company spectacles that the driver used to find the reefs.

Apparently, the spectacles had a built-in GPS in them.

Bummed out because I didn't expect the drivers to get here anytime soon, I went ahead and used some Vroom Vroom juice from the Vrenominalapsoti-ka tree.

It made my ship go buzz Buzz.

I don't mind going buzz buzz, but it's

literally not nearly as convenient as going vroom vroom.

After filling up my snazzy space cruiser and my hungry belly, I headed on out into the great wide open space, never knowing what I might find this time as I travel out into the great wide vastness before me.

Whilst traversing across the universal divide, I camst upon an ancient portal, built by my great ancestors who lives on Mechanportalonia.

It was literally their job there to make portals where they could go and transport stuff back and forth quickly.

I wondered where this one could lead.

I had heard mysterious things about the portals and where they could lead.

Maybe one would literally lead me to the mythical land of Wisconsin.

I have been told they have this stuff called Cheese, which is what cheese spread is supposedly made from.

So I zoom into the portal a little over the speed of the universal speed factor.

I knew it was risky, because my engines were made for half that speed.

Plus I knew I was pushing it with using only Vroom Vroom and not Buzz Buzz.

But I digress, because all of that is common knowledge for those of us in the know.

And I am sure you know, because I just know these things.

As I enter the portal, I experience a little shake, but that does not phase me, for I was trained to *drive by the greatest driver ever know, whose name escapes me right now, but I will let you know when* I remember, unless you already know, because the driver was the greatest.

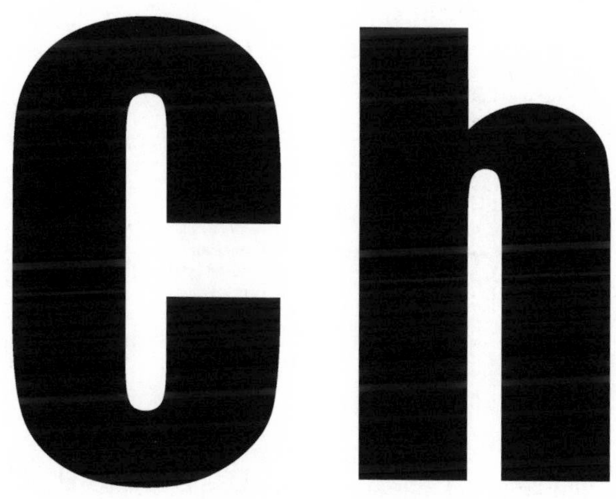

apter 6

But I digress, because all of that is common knowledge for those of us in the know.

And I am sure you know, because I just know these things.

As I enter the portal, I experience a little shake, but that does not phase me, for I was trained to drive by the greatest driver ever know, whose name escapes me right now, but I will let you know when I remember, unless you already know, because the driver was the greatest.

I say "was greatest", because the greatest driver has gone on to become the greatest wonkle berry chef this side of the Gonorbian Space Divide, which splits the universe into the right side and the east side.

And so thus I was the last apprentice of this greatest of all legends whose name escapes me even now, which is strange, being that my memory has been recorded as the best memory ever observed, having memorized the name of billions of objects and dozens of planets and the names of all the members of Nemudo since its inception.

Nemudo has had many members, in that they commonly leave after they turn 948.4 lerkins, in which they are old enough to become light captains in the greatest exploration brigade in the universe, and even the galaxy - the Great Light Captain Exploration Brigade of the Known Universe Which Explores the Unknown Universe!

As I literally get nearer to the portal, I notice a light ring around the edge.

It is literally Green.

As I am sure you know, green is the universal color for danger for all intelligent life forms.

The great universal council convinced

the lesser intelligent species it meant “go”, and that way we could have them unwittingly go into the dangerous areas for us.

When it was clear to go in for us higher forms, it would turn red, which told the lesser forms to stop and get away while us higher life forms would go, knowing that the danger is clear.

At least that is what the lesser intelligent life forms have shared with us.

They literally told the great universal council to go ahead and convince them the thing so they would think that then do the opposite when the light did the thing where it changes to the thing.

Literally.

As the light turned the brightest red ever seen, I entered the portal.

In it I saw and experienced many wonderful things, things too wonderful to explain: the lights, the sounds, the splendor, the tiny little dots floating all around, the merchants on all the corners, the streaks of light of different colors and widths and shapes and tones and height and lengths and widths, and local mariachi band playing my favorite tunes.

It was really neat.

As I near the halfway mark in the portal, I see a small passage to the east.

I think to myself “Hey, Razzie, that looks quite ominous.

Why do you think they put that small passage there?"

And then I reply, "Well, Razzie, it looks like they were trying to create an alternative route to somewhere new."

So I replied back, "Good thinking, Razzie.

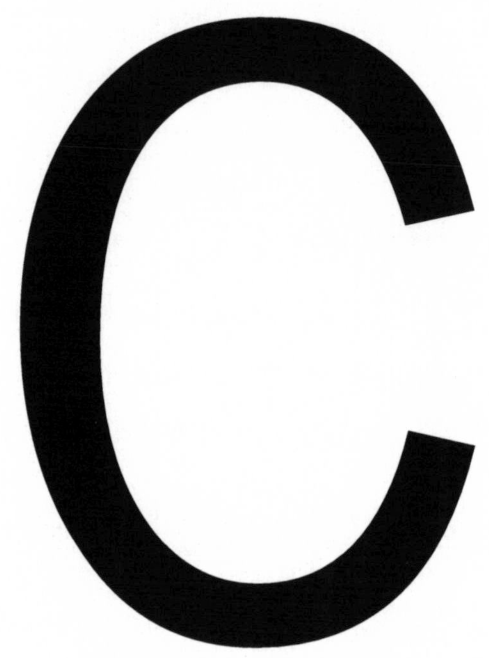

hapter 7

And so I replied back again, "Kudos.

Let's go for it!

Set the rockets on full throttle!

Into the small deviated hole that is barely visible in the portal!"

As I jam up the speed, the lights move faster, the mariachi band plays faster, the local merchants start offering bigger discounts, and I see everything moving faster.

As I start to reach the end of the vast tunnel, I can actually see the exit.

It is as beautiful as it is vast.

It is the outside space I have come to know and love.

The stars, the gaseous clusters, the asteroid, the randomly discarded microwave, balloons that escaped the orbit, big burning balls of gas, discarded quarks and gluons, and other large hydrogen burning spheres.

But then I realize I am still in the portal.

All that I am seeing is stuff stuck inside the portal - stars, the gaseous clusters, the asteroid, the randomly discarded microwave, balloons that escaped the orbit, big burning balls of gas, discarded quarks and gluons, and other large hydrogen burning spheres, all of it.

Somehow they stuck an entire universe inside the portal!

I look for a good planet to refuel, and I see this greenish blue planet stuck between a bunch of much better looking planets.

I figure that it would be a good place to rest, because no reasonable species would want to live on that planet.

But low and behold, the planet was full of creatures.

Actually, it wasn't completely full.

Most of the creatures resided on the surface area, with a wide variety dwelling in the wet part.

There was still a lot of sky and dirt where the creatures didn't live.

Actually, my most excellent observation skills noticed the dirt has really small ones, but they didn't really take up a lot of space because they were really small.

Actually.

So I landed my ship, and shrank and molded myself to look like the predominant species.

But when I realized it wasn't really the cats or dogs or the mice, I morphed myself into one of the bipedal creatures that ran around everywhere to and fro.

To and fro.

To and fro.

These creatures were really busy going to and fro.

I wonder where they are going, to and fro like that.

Eventually, my friends Dazzle and Gustov will arrive to help me study these mysterious beings.

Together, we literally work together as a super team of secret travelers who use this crusty old planet as a base for our many travels, trying to find a way home from this portal buried within a portal buried within a portal.

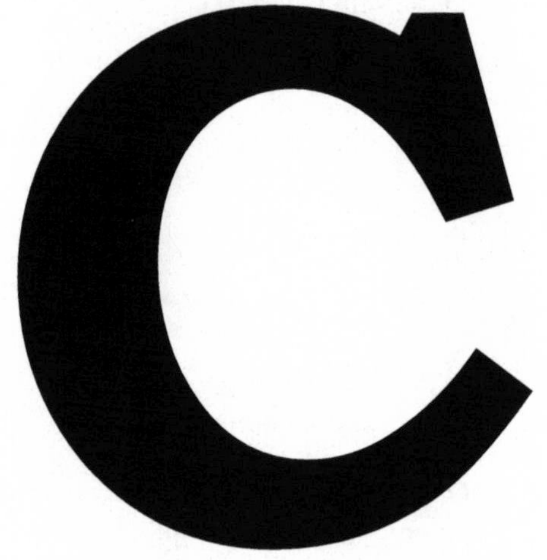

hapter 8

[Discuss how Razzle met Gornothan and how Gornothan empowered Razzle with the power to do things]

Chapter 9

Time is our friend.

We know the ins and outs of this space and time fabric, in that our ancient ancestors helped construct it in our garage.
We just need to literally find the blueprints and the mysterious objects that will help us in our grand quest.

When I landed here on this strange new planet, I needed to find a place to call home.

I looked high.

I looked low.

I looked all around.

Eventually, I would find a nice little squalor among other squalors where I could work on my inventions and gadgets.

There were many things I hoped I could accomplish.

There were many things I was hoping to do.

And it was my job to make sure the things I wanted to do was accomplish.

It's always been like that.

I have jobs to accomplish and hope to

do them in such a way that the job is accomplished.

The first thing I needed to do was find a place to stay.

The squalor among squalors was nice, but it was hard to tell how long I would remain.

It was quite mysterious, in that we never saw the owner, and we never paid any rent.

It was, however equipped with many changes of clothes and appliances, and some food that had previously been tested for safety.

So I knew the food was good.

The water still poured.

I had to hide my ship in the back room for safe keeping.

I was able to use some sheets the owners had generously left behind for me to us.

The next thing was to literally find a most excellent means of blending in.

I tried baking, professional badminton, cheese can tester, high school physics teacher, excavator, and Farrier.

But for now, I work at a temp agency so I can come and go as I need.

I have a wide array of skills, so they use me for a wide variety of excellent work when they need the highest caliber of work.

When I am not working, I use my well trained mind to develop methodologies of exploration so that if I can find a way to return home, I can find a way to transport back and forth.

I kind of like it here, but I miss the fine cuisine that is not available here.

And I need some buzz buzz

berries if I am ever going to get home.

I am Razzle Doratasmute of Galeqqis

I kind of like it here, but I miss the fine cuisine that is not available here.

And I need some buzz buzz berries if I am ever going to get home.

pilogue

[put in Lex's poem about friendship and the eternal matters]

The End?

House

Milk
Eggs
Squash
Starfruit
Kumquats
Tomatoes
Plums
Pasta
Rice
Bread
Pulses
Red kidney beans
White beans
Green lentils
Chopped tomatoes
Marmite
Soup
Hakarl
Tripe
Surstromming
Fruit, nuts, and seeds
Tuna
Salmon
Mackerel
Onions
Garlic
Fruit
Vegetables
Cooking oil
Butter
Basil
Oregano
Coriander
Cumin
Milk
Shiokara
Eggs

Mom's list

Cheese
Yogurt
Milk
Eggs
Squash
Starfruit
Stinkhead
Kumquats
Tomatoes
Plums
Pasta
Rice
Bread
Pulses
Red kidney beans
Escamol
Head Cheese
Sago
White beans
Green lentils
Chopped tomatoes
Soup
Haggis
Fruit, nuts, and seeds
Tuna

For work Tuesda

Salmon
Mackerel
Onions
Garlic
Fruit
Vegetables
Cooking oil
Butter
Basil
Oregano
Coriander
Cumin
Milk
Eggs
Cheese
Yogurt

IF YOU WOULD SAY I AM DAZZLE

By

Arsidious, The Great Writer

If you would say I am Dazzle
I would say you are right
If you said I was Harold
I would say you were not right.

For I am Dazzle
I like to bedazzle
Even if it's casual
Till the garment is cool

I enjoy warm queso
It's true cause I say so
I keep my ducks in a row
Even though I never show

Life is a gamut
Of cannot and could've
Left and then right foot
A game of shouldn't and
shouldst

I was born on the left side of the cosmos
Where dreams and vision are the most
And we've never seen a ghost
Or at least those on the coast

Changes always come
So I left from where I am from
To go where there is conundrum
And learn the beating of the drum

And learn the beating of the drum

For all I know was wrapped up
In a small shell left in a cup
Next to the shelf next to the ketchup
Never to challenge, never to disrupt

So i hope on the intergalactic train

To travel through the intergalactic rain

So I could expand my brain

Before all I knew went down the drain

Down the drain to where the drain water doth run

Down where the water never sees the sun

Full of wrappers and cups and hot cross buns

Doesn't sound like that much fun

So the train took me beyond
my scope

Through dimensional strato-
spheric envelope

On this metal antelope

To find maybe a lost garden
heliotrope

I look for a sign of where one mighst go
On my mechanical guanaco,
Drinking my Espres-so,
dance the flamenco, while singing in falsetto

While on my voyage to my destination

A mystic [something mysterious] clogged the filtration

According to my disproportionately amazing computation

It appeared to be some gregarious electromagnetic crustation

Whilst the clog slowed us down we pulled into a store

A bag of circus peanuts what what I was hunkering for

When all of a sudden, we were encroached by an angry Ichthyosaur

Fortunately, I am a trained Ichthyosaurus matador

- The Ichthyosaur swooped, the Ichthyosaur shrieked,
- Across the cosmos, the Ichthyosaur streaked
- When the Ichthyosaur took my peanuts
- I almost freaked

But when the Ichthyosaur stopped, a voice gen-
tly spoke
Please do not worry, it's not your fear I envoke
We are scouring the universe and beyond
For the last periwinkle artichoke

So I searched in my glove compartment

Where I keep items long out of print

And found the map to a lost continent

Made out of wax, string and **peppermint**

So I said to the Ichthyosaur maybe we should try here

A land full of robots and a ***buccaneer****,*

We should go before the last artichokes disappear

Eaten by a strange and silly **puppeteer**

We all jumped back on my celestial bus

For most of the ride we discussed the character of the rhombus

My friend said “I'm afraid of being superfluous

I find other polyhedrons quite simply vacuous”

With time all in <u>flusters</u>

I boosted the thrusters

I wound up the woosters

and gassed up the goosters

So I said to the Ichthyosaur maybe we should try here

A land full of robots and a **bucca-neer**,

We should go before the last arti-chokes disappear

Eaten by a strange and silly **pup-peteer**

We all jumped back on my celestial bus

For most of the ride we discussed the character of the rhombus

My friend said “I'm afraid of being superfluous

I find other polyhedrons quite simply vacuous”

We followed the map to some strange destination
A cavern in space underneath a space station
It reminded me of home, but with no correlation
I flew into the cavern with restless jactation

With lights and sounds and all sort of flash

The caverns parameters started to slapdash

In flux we went through the quantum balderdash

I worked very hard not to spill my caustic potash

We arrived to the bastion beyond the pastel gates

Were wonders and curiosities and other stuff awaits

The realm where the lost treasures are served on plates

And we look for the ancient fruit that none can obliterates

The Ichthyosaur said “hand me the twisted cactus

That bears the mark of the mystic walrus

That dwelt among the giant platypus

That kept their watch over the mystic epipactis.”

So I passed the cactus shaped like a umbonia spinosa

As the Ichthyosaur sang it [a] virtuosa

Which transformed the cactus into a gloriosa

But not like the ones found on Formosa

The gloriosas from Formosa are good,

but it was important to have one from this planet,

because the genetic make up of gloriosas from here have a unique quality that allow them to be genetically manipulated into the things that we needed them to become.

The ichthyosaur took out a transformation laser

And handed to the local appraiser

The value maker traded it for a party favor

The kind one would find on a comet or a glacier

The party favor made a hemidemisemiquaver

A note which activated a hidden quazar

That worked like a cosmic breaker

Resetting the breaker on my electric razor

With my razor reset, i said my adieu
And headed back out into the intergalactic blue
To find the place where I would eventually lay my shoe
My waffle maker, my veggie juice, and my extensive collection of lattice, too

lattice, too

As I pass the signs I must be getting close

To the place I will raise my silos

To hold my fettuccine, my squids, and my fructose

And my [some place really really unique and neat] I shall place juxtapose

And so here I am on the strange little planet

Not quite gelatinous, not quite granite

It should be a good place to explore, it won't hurt, can it?

It looks mostly harmless, not everything is volcanic.

And so I met Gustov and Razzle,

Who like to bedazzle

So we formed an exploration crew who went exploring on various exploration trips to find things.

With our unique skills, our explorations would become legendary across the universe, and even Anderson.

35 35

The End

The Eighth Book in a series of 3 Glorious trilogies!

I am called Gustov of the Gooses

By

Arsidious, The Great Writer

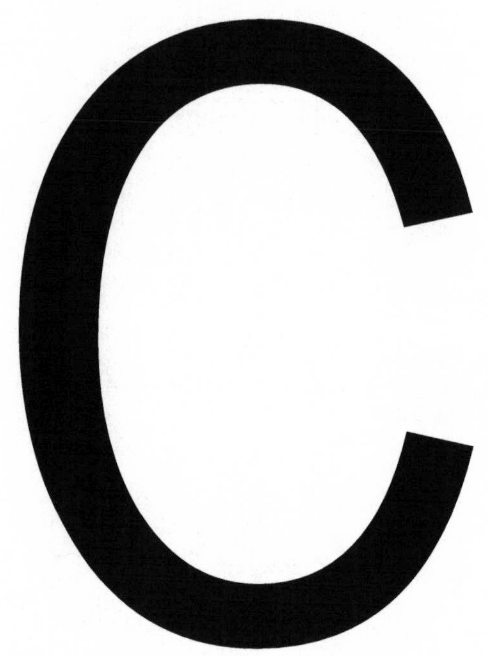

hapter 1

When they were handing out names, I told them "I am the goose of Goosatonia". And they said "We shall refer to you as Gustov Goosa." and so I am called Gustov, Gustov of the Gooses.

I like geese. On the planet I have come from, Geese are the official pets. There are puppy geese, kitty geese, pygmy marmoset geese. Geese are strong. They are smart. Smarter than a lot of people. My best friend is a goose. Gusarious Guttenaba of Goosatonia. Or Gusgutgo for short. On my planet, nicknames are typically derived by using the first or second syllable of every word.

I like the color periwinkle. It reminds me of my favorite plaid stuffed ostrich. It used to be a real ostrich, but when it flew away, I made a stuffed one out of some old rags. On my planet, all rags are officially plaid. Plaid makes us glad, as we like to say. We like plaid because we like to be glad.

There are so many things about me you would like if you knew me, because I am an easy person to like. All my friends like me. Even some of my acquaintances like me. I don't have any enemies, because that would mean someone doesn't like me, and that wouldn't make me glad. So if I find someone who might not like me yet, I give them some plaid, because plaid makes everyone glad.

One such group of people I gave some plaid to were so happy they gave me a spaceship to go exploring the universe. They said I could take as much time as I want. So I headed off to explore the universe, and even the galaxy, in my new ship my friends gave me. I thought I might find some new variations of plaid.

On place I landed had lots of lost socks and wigs. If you took some old newspapers and stuffed them in the socks, you could make your own ostrich with them. You could have an ostrich with curly hair, one with straight hair, one with wavy hair, one with crimped hair, one with really curly hair, one with straight hair, one with a bowl cut, and one with a mix of crimped hair and curls.

So now my ship is full of me and several of my ostrich friends. Tetrix, my ostrich with long straight hair with curls on the bottom had to stay behind and finish some homework for hypothetical physics II class - the lab work for it was due next Monday, and some of the team wasn't keeping up their end, which left a lot of extra work for the rest of the team.

So I and my ostrich crew head off to explore and share our love of plaid to all the domains we could find. Many places were so happy with our sharing that they helped us refuel without us repaying. Many times, they had the ship refueled and ready to go before we were even done with our multi-level sharing pyramid full of trickle down plaidness and gladness!

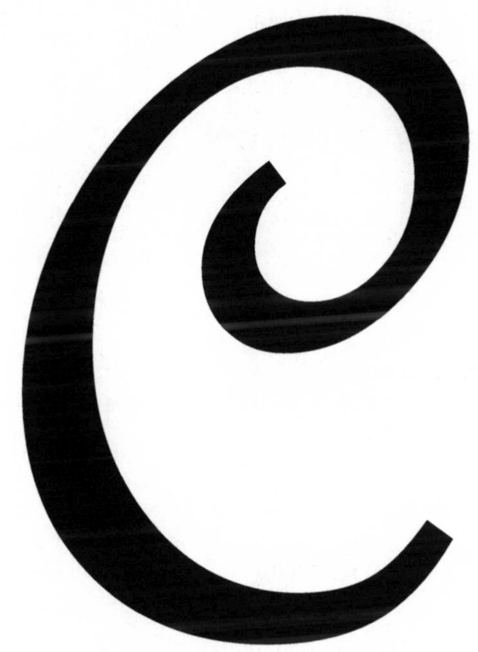

hapter 2

Some places were so full of gladness that they shared our gladness with other planets, who would let us know they already received our plaidness and didn't even need us to come share!

So much plaidness

and gladness to go

around!

But then, one planet made sure to tell me of a planet really really really really far away that no one had ever been to, where no one had ever heard of the gladness from plaid, so they gave me a map, fueled up my vehicle, and said goodbye before me and my ostrich companions even got a chance to share or explore or taste the sweet taste of the local waffles which we could smell from our spaceship, which apparently came in through the ventilation systems, which I thought weren't even in working order since I didn't really clean them regularly like I was supposed to, since the instructions said I should change them every 9million gigamiles or every 700 rotations of the smallest moon of Yedimatafadababa-sista. So after getting all the instructions, and making sure I had enough waffles for me and my crew, we headed off into space to this poor, unfortunate planet which had never experienced the gladness of plaidness. My ostrich friends were SOOOOOO excited! It would be the greatest adventure of all time and ever. We were so happy!

So me and the ostriches got on the ship and headed out. We took time during our journey to remember the friends we had met along

the way and the new ones we had picked up as we traveled.

OFF WE WENT.

Leaving was so hard, because we had such a good time, and because the gravity was very strong. But eventually, our vessel reached the velocity it needed to obtain altitude and fly into the great sea of stars.

We traveled so fast. It was unbelievable how fast we were going. We had never been this fast before, except for Ostrich passenger #57, which apparently had been on a ship that could go faster.

There were a lot of planets we passed. We could pass them fast because of the ship we were in was fast. We actually passed some other space travelers, because their ship was not as fast as ours. One was even the same make and model, but we still were going faster… it may have been the fuel we were using or the fact that my load was really light: stuffed plaid ostrich passengers don't weigh a lot. It looked like the other vehicle had a lot of luggage and passengers that weren't stuffed ostriches, which would have made for a heavier load. It could also be that I was tied to a comet, thanks to the last planet I was at. They wanted to make sure I got to the planet that was far away as fast as I could so I could share with them the gladness of plaidness.

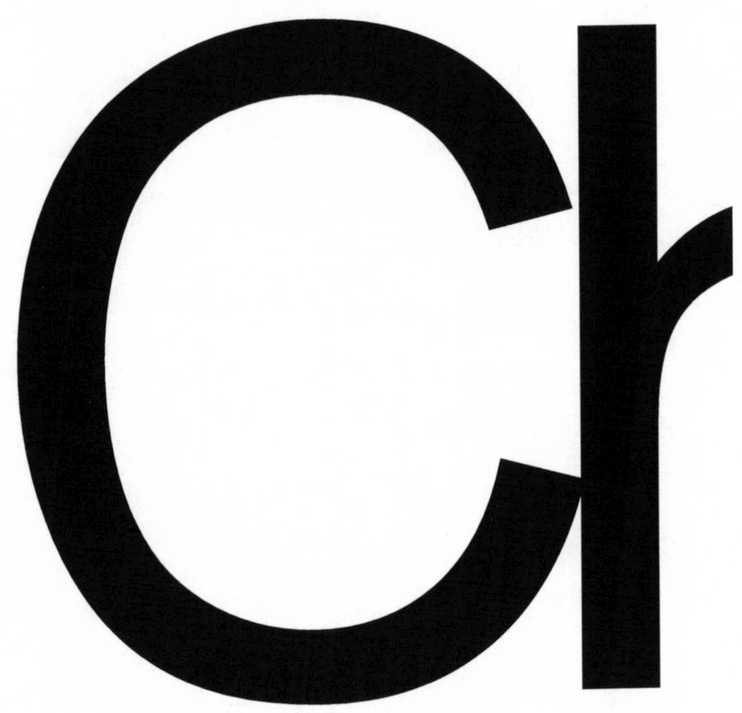

apter 3

One planet we were able to stop at had a lot of Hot Cocoa. I like hot cocoa. I also like cheese puffs and stickers.

Another planet we stopped at gave us some used tinsel. I thought it would be great to use to decorate the ship, being that there is no telling how long I will be spending on this fine vessel. Most of the tinsel was one color, but I was able to make it plaid with some marker I found under the seat and in the dash-board. I strapped several strings of the tinsel on the back of the ship and it makes it look like I am going super fast through space, like I am a comet.

Chapter 4

To get to this planet that needed my expertise in all things plaid, I had to travel through several black holes, and a couple of asteroid belts, and supernovas, and mysterious linking things that tied various locations of the universe together so I could get there before I got too old to travel.

In one such space tunnel I went through, I saw a bunch of space miners looking for some special minerals. I laughed at them and told them that space minerals only grow in the spring, and they needed to wait a few months. If they wanted to look for some intergalac-

in season. They said thank you for the information, and played some chess with my ostrich crew. After we were done with our afternoon tea, we headed back out through the tunnel. After leaving, I then remember that goldfish crackers season was coming up soon, but they needed to leave the tadpoles alone until they were fully grown.

In another Space tunnel, I met some space turtles. They were having trouble sewing their own stuffed ostriches to add to their collection because they had lost their sewing patterns. I let them borrow mine, and we were on our way again. I told the turtles just to mail them when I get my my new place on my new planet.

As we make the final turn to arrive at my new planet, one of the ostriches look as me as though wanting to say something. Then I realized the ostriches can't really speak, because they are just stuffed ostriches. So I pulled out an intergalactic stuffed animal voice modulator. It said:

> Groatinade wati morf-pha simpnod winktet lepto simphazi zizi nono jimpnei sokesa dododa bilinkinata sopsop toftof wigiwig huqhuq wizzle trigwes sinrm quiokji wjoihn wegbds ohnuh wegiuo sdfowre giierd qgtes squid gwged nubbinub-boe hruppa hruippa hrookail.

I sat there for a moment trying to decipher what it said, and then realized I needed a stuffed animal translator. So I pulled out a translator called the Scantronic Techno Ultra Pnumatically Horizontal Entergized Diametric Onological Sound Tinker Radio Inner Gammaray Translator (aka the STUPHEDOSTRIG Translator). The newer models of the intergalactic stuffed animal voice modulators have the translators built in, but this is an older model.

THe ostrich repeated again:

> Groatinade wati morfpha simpnod winktet lepto simphazi zizi nono jimpnei sokesa dododa bilinkinata sopsop toftof wigiwig huqhuq wizzle trigwes sinrm quiokji wjoihn wegbds ohnuh wegiuo sdfowre giierd qgtes squid gwged nubbinubboe hruppa hruippa hrookail.

The translation said

thanks for driving."

I said "You are most welcome."

The ostrich just stared at me.

I realized the translator was not on.

So I turned it on.

I said "Thank you."

The Translator said "

Squids don't make good lattice fences

The ostrich just stared at me.

I realized I didn't switch the polarity of the tramsafigure. So I flipped the switch.

I said "thank you."

The Translator said:

> Gnof Willog Fpenok Sorthgi Inogpe Wisnkli Dowsa Me Simpiliy Woming. Doneg Lesdtra fegenrt sorpdi huhuh bibibib lololol gritks

The ostrich still just sat there and stared at me.

Chap-

ter 7

That was when I realized I flipped the wrong switch - I switched it to stuff pleather elephants.

So I switch it again and said "thank you."

The translator started going "

gogolop tippy lipest
toftof wigiwig huqhuq
wizzle trigwes sinrm
noil linnaf pontdse
notst…"

and then it when *POOOF* in smoke. I had blown a resistor. So I went into the spare resistor closet, but didn't find anything. Then I realize I was in the spare antipasto room, where we kept the antipasto and the feather dusters. So I went to the actual spare resistor closet and pulled out a resistor. I walked all the way back down the bridge to the office, only to find out I got the wrong size. So I walked back down the hallway, making sure to go into the correct closet, and got another transistor. I walked all the way back down the breezeway, into the office, only to find I picked up the wrong brand,

and that the translator was brand specific. So I walked all the way back down the hall, into the closet, and got the correct size and correct brand. I walk all the way back and plug in the resistor.

I say "Thank you.". Nothing. I forgot to turn it back on. I turn it on.

"Thank you."

THe translator goes

FIZZY FIZZI NOWFE LIPSA IPSEM ISPEMS SORFA LINKA DO ALLOIE WALOIE NOPPA QOQKA WIKKI WIKKI WOO WOO INOGPE WISNKLI DOWSA ME SIMPILIY WOMING. DONEG LESDTRA FEGENRT SORPDI HUHUH BIBIBIB FRUMSTA.

The ostrich just sits there. It is then I realize the ostrich is stuffed. The ostrich isn't going to move, because stuffed ostriches don't move unless the ship hits a bump.

So I go back to eating my burrito and reading the morning paper.

The next thing I knew, a phantom appeared on my ship. It said the most important thing I have ever heard and that guides me through every aspect of my treacherous journey:

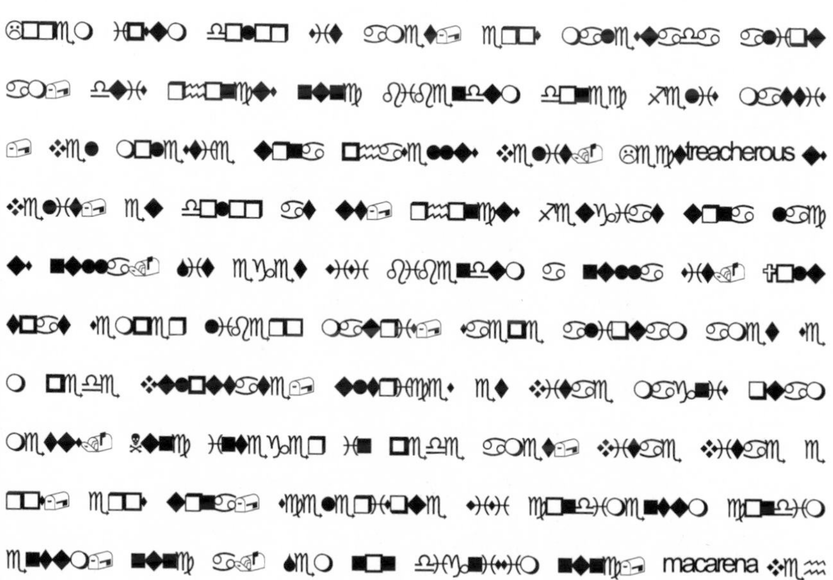

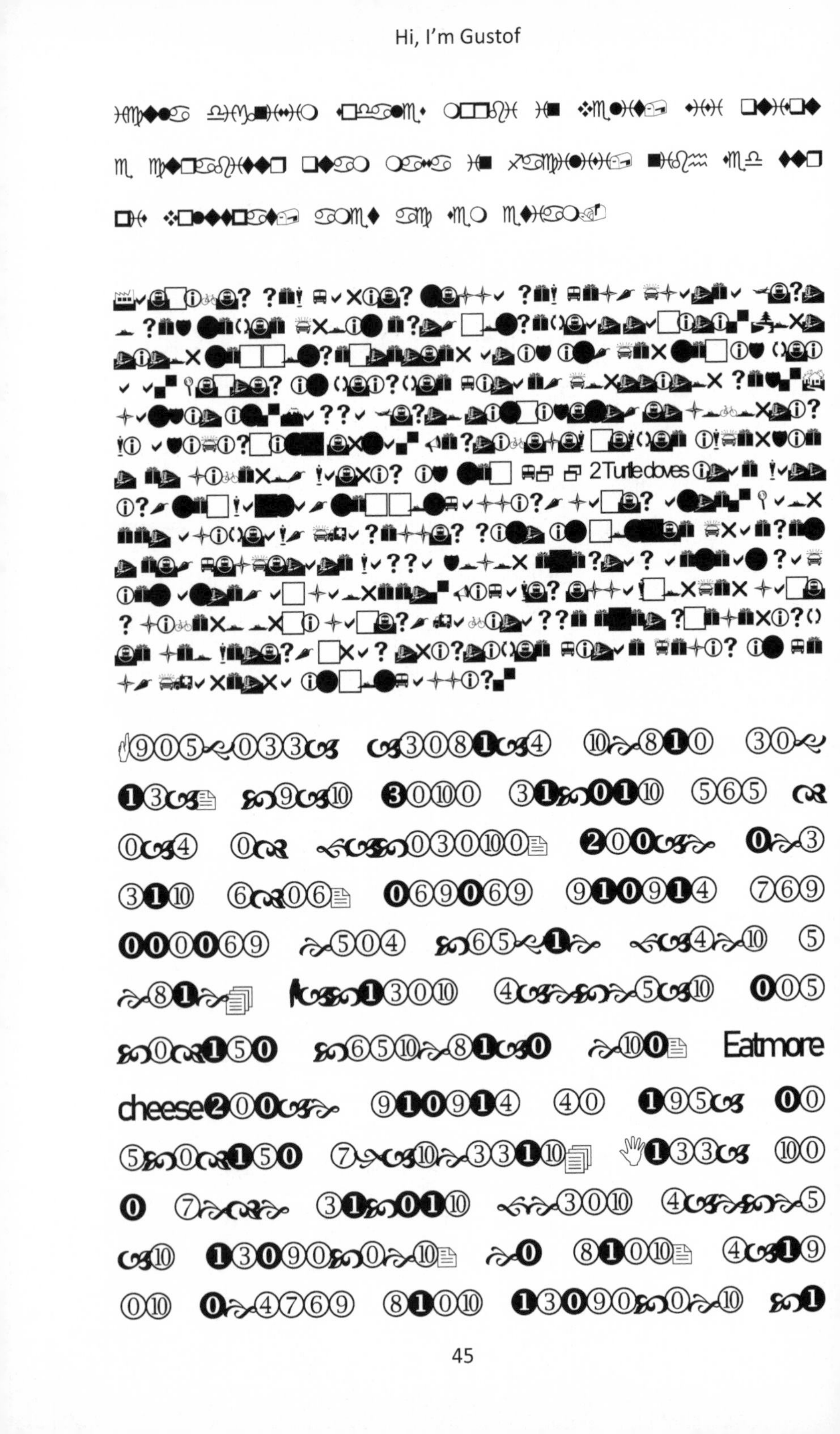

2Turtledoves

Eatmore cheese

Nascetur elit, ac in mauris nam. Ultricies ipsam nibh sed accumsan, nec ac parturient penatibus, penatibus nunc maecenas scelerisque id orci wisi. Morbi ipsum wisi suscipit eu non nec, sed aenean volutpat ut suspendisse, cras donec ligula. Felis enim, faucibus elit, dignissim nunc hymenaeos est magnis dui ut. Diam augue lorem leo a augue sed, ipsum et sollicitudin mollis tortor ac, rhoncus ligula ut, imperdiet elit commodo lacus lorem. Nulla nascetur convallis convallis, vestibulum non, elementum in. Vitae turpis dolor cras amet varius mauris, porta ut aenean parturient, at vivamus id laoreet vel, vestibulum sed suspendisse tempor fermentum, lobortis duis sagittis pellentesque parturient. Posuere neque neque lorem fermentum, quis asperiores eu nonummy, non aliquet lectus in convallis purus. Posuere lacinia nec nunc nulla ante, ante ut, vestibulum nunc, nascetur risus sodales. Fames lectus facilis vitae elit ornare, purus faucibus semper vel lectus non a. Condimentum dapibus interdum quis lobortis, non velit neque sit et dictum justo, lorem vel suspendisse.

I stood there is awe at the incredible wisdom that had just passed through my heart. Life now had new meaning. Even the ostriches stood there in awe, or at least the ones that hadn't fallen after that last space air bump we hit.

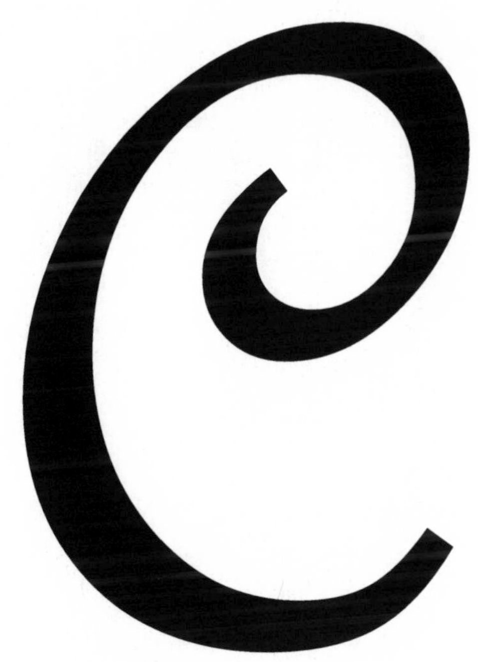

hapter 8

I said "Thank you."

Chapter 9

THe phantom just stood there and stared at me. So I looked at my translator, and realized I still had it on stuffed ostrich. I flipped it to phantom enigma, and said "thank you." again.

The phantom said "I heard you the first time. I was just in flux and trying to regain my cosmic composure so I didn't slip into an inter-dimensional vortex that is invisible to your eye, but very visible to mine, and apparently to many of your ostrich shipmates, who have kept their eye on that very vortex this entire time."

"That is one of the very reasons I have them!" I say. "They are expert vortex spotters. They have a gleam in their eye, and they spin around like they are in a tornado every time they get stuck in one."

"You are so very wise," Chrazak said.

"I must be off" said Chrazak. "There are other travelers that I must instill with my wisdom before the night is through."

"O.K." I said.

And on that note (I think a C sharp), Chrazak left the same mysterious way all phantoms leave ships in the middle of space.

With so much excitement, I got kind of sleepy. That, and the C sharp really sort of mezmerized me. So I laid down on a cot.

All of a sudden, the beeper on my ship went chartreuse and started beeping madly as though it was trying to warn me about something! So I looked out the front window! I looked out the side window! I looked out the other side window! I looked out the back window! I looked under the hatch! But I couldn't see anything! Then I realized that I still had my sleeping mask on! So I took my sleeping mask off to see that we were stuck in a tractor beam. Fortunately, for us, this was no tractor! This is a spaceship! So I kept going! ***Then*** they hit us with a spaceship beam! They pulled us down onto a landing pad! We got out! They came out and **greeted** us and said "you dropped your flowbee at the gas station. We have been trying to contact you and let you know, but you apparently were taking a nap."

I said "oh, thank you so much! The members of my crew use that to keep their feathers all nice and neat."

And then they said "but we thought they were covered with a 80/20 polyester/cotton blend."

I looked to them harshly and put my finger over my mouth to signify quiet. "Don't tell them that. They think they are real and have real ostrich feathers."

They said, "oh, we understand. We actually have a friend who would like to join your crew!" and with that they pulled out a stuffed ostrich covered in plaid 80/20 blend, just like my crew.

"By the way," they said. "The place you are looking for is right through that door over there."

I looked, and low and behold! A door! I walked through and found myself in an apartment with my new roommates, Razzle and Dazzle.

And that is the amazing story of how I got my new crew member,

ORTHAGIN GOVINU.

7He

ENd

Book Tenth

azzle, Dazzle, and Gustov in the Court of Emporai Bufant

The trilogy continues...

By

Arsidious The Great

hapter 1

"And so ends the tale of the Great Emporai Bufant's court of Lancers and Pokers of the Square Table!" Said Gustove.

"Excellent!" said Razzle.

"Yes!" Said Dazzle, "Yet I am still confused on the differences of Lancers and Pokers."

"Lancers, " said Gustov, "poke with lancers, while pokers lance with pokers."

"Ah!" Said Dazzle. "muchas gracias, my dear Gustov, for finally clearing that up for me.

"It is always my pleasure to enlighten my dear travelers with knowledge I have garnished through my many travels hither and fro, here and there, to and back again, over and over again as I travail the seven ponds and 11 land masses!"

"We always appreciate you endearing

us with your capricious knowledge and overflowing wisdom and insight." sentimented Razzle.

Yes" said Dazzle, "or as the French say, "mi burro es amarillo y tiene un horrible dolor de cabeza."

"It is knowledge like this that I have bestowed upon thee", reckoned Gustov, "that makes us wiser and empowers us to the task at hand!"

"And what task is that?" said Razzle.

"Yes, please tell!" said Dazzle. "We await to hear of the journey that waits before us!"

"Today", Gustov said with an air of majesty. "We are going to journey to the museum. For in the museum was found a note of all notes summoning all wise people to seek the door that would save Bufant's court and restore order to the land!"

"But wasn't the great court of Emporai Bufant hundreds of centuries ago, and in the distant country of Nashvilluta?" said Razzle.

"Yes, it was," said Dazzle. "Or at least I think that is what Gustove said," Dazzle said, finishing a cheese croissant, or as Dazzle called it, the Bizcocho de queso esponjoso.

"It was wiped out during the great crunchy woven wheat cracker shortage 200 years ago. When they ran out of their crunchy woven wheat cracker, they had nothing to eat their cheese wiz on, and the cheese wiz blew up one hot morning and destroyed the king-dom. The note said that the museums contained a magical door created by some trolls who built it so that people in the future could come and save their land by providing some new woven wheat crackers so they could use on the remaining cheese."

"This reminds me of a poem I wrote ," Said Dazzle.

"Let's hear it", said Gustov.

"Yes!" said Razzle.

"Horty torty,
william and gordy
Jumped the train,
even though they were 40

All they could do
was play every sporty
And josh away, josh
away all, till the pickles over ferment and
don't task like pickles any more.

So they packed up their stuff and left the grocery store and got on the trolley to head back to the flat so they could put up their lunch leftovers in their new refrigerator they were all so very proud of.

"Indubitably this is going to turn out to be the most exciting day ever!" yelled Razzle.

"I CAN HARDLY WAIT FOR ANOTHER MI-

NUTE!" shouted Dazzle. "IT"S LIKE THE MINUTES ARE GOING TRICKLY WICKLY DOWN A GIANT CLOCK SET ON A MOMENTOUS MOUNTAIN CALLED SIXTY SECOND MOUNTAIN!"

"I think my sandwich would have been better if I had the spicy brown mustard!" Screams Gustov.

hapter 2

So while riding their bikes home from the trolley stop, they made sure to stop completely at every stoplight, because they knew the importance of being safe drivers. At the last stop, Dazzle said "did anyone see that tree on the right move?"

"No! " said Razzle.

"I did not either!" said Gustov.

"Maybe it was just my *mafaufau valea playing tricks on me again." said Dazzle.*

"Or," said Razzle all of a sudden. "Maybe it was that wizard hiding behind the pole I just saw peaking out!"

Everybody turned to look.

"Thee hast tasted the winter wind, and thee knowest the bitterest season of yesterday's rummage sale." said the wizard from the pole.

The Final Book that Explains everything!

Welcome to Charlie's House

By

Arsidious, The Great Writer

3rd

Chapter 1

My name is Charlie, I don't drive a Harley, I drive a Heli, through the airy.

I am glad we have met. You seem like a nice person, just like my new neighbors: Razzle, Dazzle, and Gustov. Each one of them arrive in their own unique and individual way, different than the other, so as to not arrive at the same, giving them each a story that is just about them and not like the others.

I have lived here in Anderson for a long time. How long? I don't know. If I knew, I would have said something like how I have lived in Anderson for, lets say, 30-75 years, if that was possible. It would definitely be a larger number, not like 1 or 2, unless people didn't live here in Anderson on average of only 6 months. Then 2 years would seem like an eternity. But I am going under the assumption that most people here live here for more than 6 months. I probably haven't lived here less than 3-25, because I would still have areas of my life where I would need to acclimate myself, unless everything is exactly the same and the weather doesn't change. Then just being here a short time would be enough to acclimate one's self.

Razzle, Dazzle, and Gustov have been here less than that, because I was here when they moved here… or arrived… however you want to describe them here. This is all assuming they didn't live here prior to me moving here, and then left, so it just looked like they just moved here when really they had been here before and the town was really an old hat.

You know sometimes how you just get a feeling about someone when you meet them? Like you bump against them, and you get wet because they were in the rain, and you realize they are the type of person that gets wet when they are in the rain without an umbrella? And even umbrellas don't help you in every rain, because if there is wind, the rain goes sideways and gets you wet from every angle regardless of the umbrella. At that point, you need a good heavy poncho and a nice pair of galoshes.

Well, I had that kind of feeling when I first met Razzle, Dazzle, and Gustov for the first time. Almost as soon as I met them, I knew it would be a wild and crazy ride. Mostly because they were still trying to figure out how to fly their ship when I got on board. Apparently Gustov left a ship on the other side of a portal door. Razzle traded a ship in for some pop rocks, and Dazzle's ship was traded in for this monstrosity, because it was the only ship left from the collision.

Razzle arrived here first. Razzle's ship was much smaller. I am assuming Razzle's home planet was much smaller. But Razzle could mutate into a human size.

Dazzle arrived next. Dazzle's ship was hidden inside the apartment and disguised as a china cabinet. Dazzle was quite disoriented from the arrival and continued to speak in rhyme.

When GUstov fell from the sky, the other two had already claimed their room and side of the dining table. So Gustov had to take whatever remained. The Ostrich crew didn't really need a side of the table, because they were never very hungry. They just sat there and stared as Gustov went around and tried to make everything look plaid by drawing grids on everything and using various toners to give stuff a plaid appearance. Gustov said the plaid tones made the Ostriches feel more at home and relieved some internal angst and anxiety.

When Razzle first arrived, we toured around town. I took Razzle to the most interesting places in my town: the land dump. Razzle was thrilled because it contained all the parts needed to build intricate machineries for exciting adventures. I also took Razzle to the water recycling plant, because it was important to recognize all the things that went in to making water palatable and drinkable and safe. Razzle really appreciated that! Razzle understood the necessity for proper water treatment and storage to keep one healthy and on the go!

The next place we went was to a secret storage facility, where ancient aliens store various technological tools, like left handed water sprinklers and stow away air mattresses that you can stow away while they are still inflated.

All in all, Razzle and I had a good time looking at everything.

Then Dazzle came. At first, I took Dazzle to see the town. Razzle was busy straightening the pad up, because we didn't know how long Dazzle was planning to stay. I took Dazzle to try our famous Waffle House, but Dazzle's favorite thing was the giant slide in the middle of the town park. Unfortunately, there is no town park, and the people who owned the house were the slide was were not happy. But then I explained how Dazzle came from outer space, and they were very happy to let Dazzle experience a great playground set. The swingset was well calibrated. The sand container was very clean. Overall, Dazzle was impressed with everything.

After we got back, Razzle joined us. We went to the local fast food fine dining and grabbed some various cuisines. Both Razzle and Dazzle were surprised that their food came with such interesting objects that they could use in their spacecraft, including squeakers and squakers.

When Gustov came, it was a whole nother story. Gustov was in love with everything within sight. Gustov loved the local park, the fine cuisine, the ancient alien store, and the water treatment facility. Everything put a twinkle in Gustav's eyes.

Overall, I think it was a greatest experience for all of us. I hope they stay. I hope soon they will let me go on adventures with them. I did apologize for the incident, and know they said they forgive me. I just hope they let me go with them soon, before the mother ship comes and I have to return home.

My favorite experience with them is when

[here we need to introduce Charlie's dog or something like that]

[Maybe discuss the time Razzle wanted to go home but everyone begged Razzled to stay

[A great memory]

[take time to reflect on when Dazzle forgot the thing and the eternal conse-quences]

[wrap it up with
a big surprise]

The end

Made in the USA
Monee, IL
18 December 2019